SHE ASKED
CRAZY HORSE
WHY

Kathy Day Faulkner

SHE ASKED CRAZY HORSE WHY

ISBN 978-1-7366787-0-1

To my husband, Emmett,
and many friends
who patiently edited my work
and proffered sage advice

CRAZY HORSE

CRUNCH CRACK... CRUNCH CRACK... **CRUNCH CRACK!**

Lone Moon's muscles tensed. She knew that sound well. Crackling dead leaves and branches snapping on the trail meant a horse and rider were approaching. Was an enemy Crow warrior planning a sneak attack on the horse herd? Her heart hammered in her chest. She was out of earshot from camp. No one would hear her scream.

Lone Moon dove into thick chokecherry bushes for cover. Peeking through new green leaves and leftover clusters of dried cherries, her keen black eyes detected a lone rider on a paint horse, ambling toward her. She recognized the resolute look on his face and the red-tailed hawk feather trailing behind his flowing chestnut hair. It was Crazy Horse!

Leaping into the clearing she yelled, "Cousin! You're finally back. I've missed you!"

"*Aiyee*! Lone Moon. You almost scared the spots off my pony! What are you doing so far from camp by yourself?"

"Looking for cattails. I need their fluff to make a

doll for our new baby. Remember, it will be born during the cold moons. But where have you been? Why were you gone so long?"

"Questions, questions, so many questions," Crazy Horse said with a quiet grin. He threw one lithe leg over his horse's mane and slid down, landing lightly on both feet. He removed a rawhide leather pouch that was tied around his waist.

"I brought you something," he said, pausing to untangle a chokecherry twig from one of her unruly braids before shaking open his pouch. "Close your eyes and hold out your hand." Hundreds of porcupine quills and several glossy elk teeth spilled into her open palm. "Your grandmother can help you dye these quills different colors and sew them and the elk teeth onto your buckskin ceremonial dress."

Lone Moon's eyes shot open and her face radiated excitement as she sorted through the items in her hand. "*Pilamiyaye* (thank you) Cousin," she said, laying a hand over her heart.

These are really nice. It must have taken you a lot of time to find such perfect porcupine quills and to pull out teeth from an elk you shot."

"Nothing's too good for you, young cousin. Besides, I want you to please the spirits at the next Sun Dance," Crazy Horse said.

Lone Moon's thoughts skipped to a daydream, in which she imagined dancing at the Sun Dance wearing her fancy decorated dress. She envisioned herself bobbing up and down with elk teeth clattering in time with drumbeats while her colorful porcupine quills flashed in the sunlight, her feet floating with lilting flutes.

Crazy Horse's paint horse impatiently pawed the earth, bringing Lone Moon back to reality. She noticed a despondent look on Crazy Horse's face. "Why didn't you come back sooner? You seem sad. What happened?" Lone Moon asked.

Crazy Horse, normally optimistic, spoke in a gloomy voice, "Oh, Lone Moon, how can I explain it? It's hard for me to understand." He took a labored breath and continued. "Years ago, our Lakota people signed a treaty stating that if we let the *wasicu* (white people) build and use what they call the Oregon Trail through Lakota territory, we would not be bothered in any other way.

But now, white soldiers are directly violating this treaty by starting to build more forts equipped with troops of men who are outfitted with big guns and horses. *Wasicu* are traveling on this trail towards the setting sun, bringing lots of oxen, mules, cattle, and wagons full of supplies. We call it their *Holy Trail* because it seems so important to them. They kill buffalo, elk, and deer, leaving us with less food and fewer hides to make our clothes, moccasins, and tipis."

Lone Moon squinted in confusion, "But... why?"

"I don't know why. But enough of this sad tale," said Crazy Horse, noting the worried look on his cousin's face. "Come on. I'm starving!" he said. "Let's see how fast we can get back to camp." Crazy

Horse leaped on his horse faster than a startled frog. Reaching down and grabbing Lone Moon's arm, he swooped her sturdy body up behind him.

They galloped away at full speed, laughing at the wind pestering their faces. Lone Moon clutched her bag full of cattail fluff and the pouch from Crazy Horse close to her chest. He slowed his horse to a walk before entering the Lakota camp. Shouts of greeting and joy arose when people recognized Crazy Horse. Lone Moon tried to appear humble, but she couldn't suppress the huge grin spreading across her face. Tears started in her eyes. She was so honored to ride behind this great warrior. She slid off his horse's rump and joined all the people who had gathered around, welcoming him home.

The men hailed Crazy Horse with big smiles and claps on his back. They were relieved to see him back safely, yet anxious to go into council and hear the report about his scouting trip. Some women, knowing Crazy Horse must be hungry, quickly brought him a bowl of hot buffalo stew. He thanked them before eating it then strode away to the council tipi.

Lone Moon's mother, Morning Star, along with other women of the band treated Crazy Horse with special tenderness and care. Lone Moon guessed it was because Crazy Horse's mother had died when he was a young boy. She wondered if that was why he was quiet and soft spoken, and why he frequently went off by himself for days at a time to think and pray.

Lone Moon knew Lakota people considered Crazy Horse a leader and courageous warrior. He seemed more concerned about the tribe's future than his own glory. Because he usually scouted by himself and retreated to meditate alone, he seemed full of wisdom though still a young man. People called him a silent hero, since he never bragged about his accomplishments. Lone Moon treasured another side of Crazy Horse, who was more like her older brother. He was a teaser, pulling silly pranks on her. But mostly she liked how he treated her as an equal. She appreciated how he would give her a truthful answer no matter what question she asked him. And he listened to her dreams and worries without interrupting or giving advice.

Lone Moon reluctantly realized she would have no more time alone with Crazy Horse until he and the council had debated his strategy on how to stop the encroaching *wasicu*. In Lakota way, each person would have a chance to speak and be heard. One individual would not make an important decision that involved everybody.

Lone Moon's thoughts were jumbled as she trudged through trampled grass to the family tipi. The setting sun felt warm through her buckskin dress and shimmered on her shiny, jet-black hair. A flaming arrow of anger shot through her brain. *Life before soldiers came to Lakota territory was carefree and fun. Now the adults seem worried and upset over the smallest things. Surely, the council will come up with a good plan.*

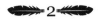

FAMILY TIME

WHEN LONE MOON entered the tipi, her grandmother, Yellow Bird, sensed something was amiss. Trying to cheer her granddaughter she said, "Oh, I'm glad you're back. Did you get cattail fluff for the doll we are making?"

In Lakota tradition, Lone Moon's grandparents lived with her family and helped in many ways. "I have the buckskin doll body stitched with buffalo sinew, so you can stuff it with soft fluff. Then if you braid some horsehair you pulled from your pony's tail, we will make the doll some long black braids like yours."

"Cloud didn't like me pulling hair out of his tail. But when I told him it was for the baby, he was okay," laughed Lone Moon, catching her grandmother's cheery mood. "And look what Crazy Horse brought me!" She emptied the rawhide pouch filled with porcupine quills and elk teeth. "*Unci*, (Grandma) will you help me cut and dye these quills for my dancing dress?"

"Of course, dear one. This morning I extracted beautiful yellow pigment from dandelions, and

I have vermillion and blue dye in my bag. From those three hues we can mix many other shades, any color you want."

"What do you think the baby's name will be?" Lone Moon's juvenile mind had already skipped to a new thought.

"Well, I hope it's Plenty Moons," joked Yellow Bird. "You realize you are called Lone Moon because you are an only child."

"Yes, but I would have three brothers if they hadn't died before they were born."

"I pray every day that this baby will survive, and you will have a brother or sister," her grandmother said in a soft voice.

"I do want a brother or sister. I don't like being an only child."

Sensing *Unci* was softening Lone Moon asked, "Can't we put a face on this doll, since it's for the baby?"

"You know we Lakota are humble and modest. Our people believe children should honor their own unique gifts given by the *Creator*. Every face is pretty in its own way, and one is not better than another. Gazing at our reflection in ponds or putting beautiful faces on dolls is a waste of time. Whoever the doll belongs to can imagine how her face looks."

"But, what if..." Lone Moon was silenced by Yellow Bird's stern look.

After supper, Lone Moon curled up on a soft buffalo hide next to her *ina,* (mother) and watched her quietly beading by firelight.

"I'm going to stay awake until *até* comes home," Lone Moon asserted.

"It may be a long while before your father is done with the council meeting. You better close those tired eyes and get some sleep," Morning Star said, patting the top of Lone Moon's head. "But first, put your hand on my belly and feel the baby's tiny feet kicking."

Lone Moon giggled when she felt a hard nudge. "It must be a strong one," she said with a grin.

"Yes, it certainly can kick," laughed Morning Star. "Now, you go to sleep, sweet girl."

Lone Moon snuggled inside her buffalo robes, listening to the familiar sound of coyotes howling. It was an eerie sound, but she felt safe and wasn't afraid. Her thoughts went to babies, and she wondered if her *até*, Sky Eagle, had secretly hoped for a boy when she was born. *He treats me like a son sometimes. It might be fun to be a boy and play war, learn to hunt buffalo, and take care of warriors' horses. I can already run faster and ride horseback better than most boys my age. But my ina wants me to spend more time learning the ways of good Lakota women.*

Lone Moon's last thought before drifting off to sleep was hoping Crazy Horse would have time tomorrow to demonstrate how to shoot grasshoppers with the small bow and arrows her *até* had given her.

➤ 3 ◀

GRASSHOPPERS AND HOOPS

"QUICK, DRAW YOUR arrow. There's a big one!" Crazy Horse encouraged.

Flustered, Lone Moon neglected to remember all the techniques Crazy Horse had taught her such as: gripping the bow; stringing an arrow; keeping her elbow straight; aiming; drawing back with a slow, steady breath; then gently releasing the arrow to find its target. In her eagerness to shoot the grasshopper, her edgy fingers pulled the arrow back lightning fast. Instead of the arrow making the intended *Whang* sound, it nose-dived into the dirt a few feet in front of her. She watched the grasshopper bound away into deep grass.

"I'll never get one," Lone Moon complained, her dark eyebrows puckering in irritation. "Grasshoppers are too quick."

"That's okay, impulsive one, you need a little more practice. See if you can shoot through this hoop when I roll it by."

Lone Moon scrunched her face, knitted her eyebrows together, and mashed the tail end of one braid in her pouty mouth. "That's harder yet. The boys make shooting arrows look easy."

"Keep practicing, and by the time I come back from raiding Crow horses, you'll be a better shooter than any boy."

"What! You're leaving again?"

"You know our tribe is low on good mounts, and the Crows have some fine horses. I may find you a new colt," Crazy Horse said. "But let's go fishing for a while before I leave."

Lone Moon's eyes sparkled. "Okay. I bet I'll catch the most trout this time. But I don't like feeling slimy worms, and grasshoppers spit icky brown juice on my hands, so you have to put them on my hook."

"Perhaps you'll get lucky and catch more fish, but I doubt it," Crazy Horse teased.

He almost always won. *Even fish are attracted to him*, Lone Moon laughed to herself.

Sitting on a grassy pond bank with their fishing strings dangling in deep water, Lone Moon smiled. She relished this time with her cousin. They could talk or enjoy being quiet together, listening to soft sounds of nature: whispering pine treetops soughing in the breeze; burbling pops of tadpoles; or melancholy hooting of doves.

It wasn't long before a question darted into Lone Moon's mind. "I heard some young braves talking about going on a *hanbleceya* (vision quest). Why do they do that? And what happens?"

"Well, most young men want to have an experience that will give direction and meaning to their adult life. They find an isolated spot and spend three or four days there alone with no food or water. They do lots of praying, seeking to learn more about the spirit world and to gain a better understanding of how we are one with all two-legged, four-legged, and winged creatures. After receiving a vision, a young man will go directly to elders, who interpret the meaning of his experience, advise him, and sometimes change his name.

"Did you go on a *hanbleceya* when you were younger?" Lone Moon asked.

"Of course. That's when I received my adult name. Before that I was called Curly."

"Would you please tell me about it?" Lone Moon probed, knowing he preferred not to talk about himself.

"Okay, little cousin, only for you," Crazy Horse relented. "In my *hanble*, (vision) I saw a pond, much like this one. A mighty Lakota warrior rose out of the pond during a powerful storm with fierce lightning flashing all around and jarring thunder crashing louder than twenty drums. This warrior was riding a horse that kept changing colors. He rode through a hail of enemy arrows and bullets without being harmed."

"That's why you paint hailstones and lightning on your face and chest before you go into battles?"

"Yes, but there's more. After many winter counts and battles in which he didn't get hurt, this warrior was stabbed after scuffling with some of his own people and white soldiers, who wanted to put him in jail. He died soon afterwards from the serious wounds."

"Was that warrior you?" Lone Moon asked timidly.

Crazy Horse nodded with a faraway stare.

"What happened after you shared your *hanble* with elders?"

"They told me I would become a leader of men and a fierce warrior who couldn't be killed in battles. My father gave me his own name, TaSunke Witko, (Crazy Horse) and he took the name, Worm."

Lone Moon chewed on her already short thumbnail, trying to make sense of his story. "Then what?"

"The vision changed my life in ways that are hard to put into words. I now deeply trust spirits are always protecting and guiding me."

"How would I know if spirits are talking to me?"

"Listen closely to those quiet voices within your heart, Lone Moon, especially in a troubling situation." Crazy Horse gazed into space. He spoke no more.

Lone Moon laid back and stared into a limitless azure sky. She noticed a cloud rising that looked like a large floating eagle feather. *I've never seen a cloud like that before. I wonder what it means? Maybe it's a sign that good things are going to happen.*

Airy bits of cotton from a cottonwood tree floated down like snow. One puff tickled Lone Moon's nose and made her sneeze. Gentle whispering of leaves lured her into a light sleep.

A fish splashing in the pond woke Lone Moon. Directly above her head, a spider clung to its web string. Without thinking, Lone Moon whacked the spider, watched it tumble down, and crushed it flat with her fist. Then she panicked.

Oh no, she thought, *what have I done?*

"Thunder Beings have killed you!" Lone Moon hastily said to the lifeless spider. Her *ina* had taught her to say this phrase if she accidently killed a spider, otherwise bad things might happen to her family. The Lakota believed Thunder Being spirits were more powerful than spider spirits and could do whatever they pleased, so she could blame them for the spider's death.

"Whew," Lone Moon stumbled back and sagged against a tree trunk. "Now, I know my family is safe. I'll try to remember not to smash a spider next time one startles me."

Crazy Horse was snoring. He hadn't heard a thing.

Eyeing her sleeping cousin, she had a sneaky thought.

"Hey, maybe I will win the contest," Lone Moon grinned mischievously. She stealthily snatched her fishing pole and cast its string to the very spot where the fish had jumped.

━━4━━

FIRST WASICU SIGHTING

"BE CAREFUL AND come back soon," Lone Moon said handing Crazy Horse a small rawhide pouch made of decorated elk hide and filled with buffalo berries she had picked especially for him.

"I have to return soon. Who else would have enough patience to teach you how to shoot your bow?" Crazy Horse joked with a slight grin on his painted face.

She gave him a lopsided grin that didn't really hide her fear. She worried every time he went on horse raids of neighboring Crows and Pawnees. She feared he would get hurt, or worse, never return at all.

Families lined up to see the warriors off, cheering for them to bring back lots of horses. They knew Crazy Horse would give most of his share of horses to any widows or elderly people who had no one to provide for them. Crazy Horse had painted his body and horse with sacred designs, attached a red hawk feather to his long brown hair, and tied a small black stone behind his left ear. He believed these rituals would shield him from all danger and provide him with safety.

Lone Moon's heart sang with relief when she saw her *lala* (grandfather), Swift Deer, getting in line behind Crazy Horse and the other men. She knew he would protect the warriors from danger because he was a medicine man who could say powerful prayers and tend to any injuries that might happen. She smiled as her *lala* rode by, looking so honorable, dressed in his bone breastplate and deer skin leggings edged with fringes that hung below his moccasin-clad feet. A grizzly bear skin was draped over his back with the bear head and teeth protruding over his brown, weathered face. When he saw Lone Moon, his bright eyes twinkled in tenderness, and his thin lips spread into a big smile as if to reassure her he would look after Crazy Horse.

Crazy Horse, leading the warriors, rode his splendid black and white horse. Watching the group trot away, Lone Moon prayed to the *Creator* to keep them safe. *I feel bad that my até hurt his knee, but I'm kind of glad he can't go on the raid. One less person to worry about.*

She sat on her beloved pony, Cloud, and watched until the raiding party was out of sight. The pony's name stemmed from a white cloud-shaped spot on his brown rump. Cloud was her best pal but was starting to show some age. Lone Moon didn't want to think about it but knew Cloud would have to be replaced one day. *Maybe that's why Crazy*

19

Horse talked about bringing me a young colt, she thought.

When she returned home, her parents were discussing a possible visit to the Brule band led by Conquering Bear. "I would really like to visit my relatives," Morning Star said. "It's been a long time since I've seen them. They are camped only a few sleeps away near the *wasicu* soldier camp at Fort Laramie, waiting for their rations promised them by the treaty."

"Okay, we can go camp with them for a while," Sky Eagle responded. "The time away will give my knee a chance to heal."

"Will I go, too?" interrupted Lone Moon, her face bright with anticipation. "I've never seen the Fort or a *wasicu.*"

"Of course," Sky Eagle said, "the whole family will go. I can take hides I've skinned to exchange for things we need at the nearby trading post. Your mother and grandmother will have a chance to visit their Brule relatives, and you can get re-acquainted with them. They haven't seen you since you were four winter counts. And look at you now; you have survived ten winters."

"There's much work to be done to prepare for our trip," Morning Star said. "Lone Moon your *unci* and I need you for tipi take down. You can help load it on pony drags along with everything else we need for the journey."

Lone Moon was too excited to protest. Her mind was bursting, speculating what new things she'd see, relatives she'd meet, and the beads, colorful blankets, dyes, and pretty cloth her father might trade for his hides. And she couldn't wait to sleep on open prairies and watch stars unfold their stories.

Two sleeps later, the family was winding into a valley on horseback when they caught sight of Fort Laramie bordered on three sides by a horse-hoof shaped river. When they rode closer, Lone Moon's eyes snapped wide open and her mind spun in surprise at so many buildings, people, animals, and activities. Soldiers dressed in blue clothes were either riding prancing horses, driving wagons filled with supplies, marching in rows, carrying long guns that reflected sunlight, or milling around odd-shaped tents and long, wooden buildings. Cows, oxen, and mules chewed on piles of dead grass in a corral, and horses neighed complaints to each other. Goats and sheep wandered throughout the unruly mess. Lone Moon heard loud, coarse voices of men, women talking in a shrill, strange tongue, and children shouting as they chased barking dogs. The soldiers had hairy faces and wore funny hats. The women wore long skirts that billowed out and dragged in the dry dirt. Smells of cookfire smoke mingled with a stinky odor of fresh manure. There were big wagons, with rounded white tops, pulled by huge oxen and filled with families spilling out all sides. Some of these wagons were fording the wide river and swayed dangerously in the swift currents. Dust wrapped everything in a haze but Lone Moon could still see the large piece of red, white, and blue cloth suspended from a tall pole. Her father drew her attention to one man who seemed different than the rest.

"See how his hat's brim is turned up on one side with a fancy feather attached? Last time I was here, the fur trader told me his name is Lieutenant Grattan."

Lone Moon felt confused after witnessing these bizarre sights and sounds. She plied her *até* with questions: "Why do the soldiers march in straight lines? Do they ride all those strange animals in the corrals? Why do those animals eat dead grass? Why do men have hair on their faces? Can women ride horses in those long skirts? Who do all the children belong to? Are those wagons like our pony drags? How do they keep them from tipping over when they cross the river?"

"Hold on, Lone Moon. I can't answer all those questions at once," laughed Sky Eagle.

"But, do all the soldiers bring their families to this fort?"

"No, only the important soldiers. There isn't enough room for all of them to come. Many soldiers have to leave their families at home for long periods of time."

"That must be sad for the children to have their fathers away. I miss you when you're only gone a few sleeps for a hunt."

She decided the *wasicu* weren't that much different than her own people. *The soldiers have families and are husbands, fathers, brothers, and sons. And the children laugh, roll hoops, and play with dogs, like I do.*

Her father, wanting to quash any more questions, said, "Last one to the Brule camp is a spotted frog!" He kicked his horse into a lope. Lone Moon raced close behind him but couldn't catch him. He slowed to a walk and waited for her, reminding Lone Moon they should approach the camp with dignity. Lone Moon's heart flooded with anticipation when she spied a big circle of tipis. The many questions spurred by the fort scene streamed behind her, unanswered.

As quickly as bees flash among flowers, Morning Star, Yellow Bird, and Lone Moon set up their tipi inside the Brule encampment, unloaded pony drags, and put a kettle of water filled with dried buffalo meat on the fire for supper. Lone Moon was introduced to many relatives, who came to welcome them. She knew it was disrespectful for her to address an older person by his or her name. Instead, she greeted them as grandmother, grandfather, uncle, auntie, or cousin. *I'm glad I don't have to memorize all their names,* Lone Moon reflected.

Some cousins close to her age surged around her and asked her to play. *This visit is going to be more fun than I imagined,* Lone Moon thought as she chased after them.

5

THE MORMAN COW RUINED
EVERYTHING

LONE MOON SAT with her Miniconjou cousin,
High Forehead, decorating their bows with
hawk feathers and colored strings of rawhide.
Holding up her bow and smiling with satisfaction,
Lone Moon said, "Thanks for showing me how to
make mine look like a real warrior's weapon."

But High Forehead was distracted by a loud ruckus
and didn't answer. Lone Moon's eyes followed his
fixated gaze and saw barking dogs racing after a
lame cow with sticky-out ribs. They watched as the
dogs surrounded the cow, growling and snapping
at her heels. Saliva dripped from their bared fangs.
The terrified animal whirled and kicked. She broke
free of the dogs' circle and ran berserk. Dazed by
strange surroundings, the irrational cow crashed
into a drying rack of deer meat and trampled some
fleshing tools, which clattered and spooked her
more.

"Look out!" shouted High Forehead, shoving
Lone Moon aside. "It's coming right at us!"

The manic cow careened into the tipi, almost

stomping on their little cousin, Small Bird, who was napping inside.

"Aiyee!" screamed Small Bird, bolting out of the tipi right into Lone Moon's arms.

High Forehead, following the yipping dogs, strung his bow and chased after the frenzied cow. Lone Moon shushed Small Bird's cries, assuring her it would be okay. Their mothers came running to make sure the girls were safe and held them in a protective hug.

They watched the panicked cow romp through the camp, upsetting and scattering everything in her path. People ran out of their tipis yelling and waving arms and blankets to deter the unruly animal from any more destruction. The exhausted cow finally stopped. Foam oozed from her mouth, her sides heaved, and her eyes bulged with fright. Once again, brutish dogs surrounded her, woofing and snarling, but she was too spent to move. High Forehead, taking ragged breaths, fumbled to draw his sharp arrow back but deftly planted it behind the cow's foreleg, straight into her heart. She slumped to the ground.

People stood with their mouths agape, trying to register what had just happened. High Forehead, bent over at his waist, inhaled gulps of air. It wasn't long before women from High Forehead's family collected themselves, unsheathed their sharp knives, and butchered the cow where she lay. They salvaged as much meat as possible, although it was tough, stringy, and nothing like tender cuts of young buffalo. It's flea-bitten hide, hardly worth the effort to clean and tan, was kept for some future use.

The next morning, Lone Moon listened as everyone rehashed the cow incident. She overheard Sky Eagle telling Morning Star that the cow had escaped her tether at the Mormon camp near Fort Laramie. He said because it had been so hot yesterday, the cow had probably wandered into the Brule camp, searching for water. Lone Moon wondered what her father meant when he said this cow incident might start big trouble with the white soldiers.

Several young men thought the whole event was rather comical. They joked and teased High Forehead.

"Hey, hey, there's the big brave hunter who shot a decrepit old cow," Walking Bull laughed, pointing at High Forehead.

"You must have been so frightened," teased Wolf Ears.

High Forehead smiled at their jokes, but defended himself, "My family is hungry. We're not getting the meat that was promised from the Fort. The white soldiers took our guns and horses, so we can't hunt our own meat when we need it."

Crazy Horse had told Lone Moon that some Lakota people lived on reservations near the Fort because they were guaranteed free rations and meat if they gave up their guns. "These people think doing what the *wasicu* want will bring peace.

But my warriors and I don't trust the white men and are disgusted with these loafers from various tribes who seem to be looking for an easier way to live."

Lone Moon was glad her *até* chose to live with Crazy Horse's band, so her family could still roam free, hunting anytime they wished.

Camp activities resumed their normal routine, and most everyone dismissed the cow incident. Yellow Bird, Morning Star, and Lone Moon joined other women and girls, who were picking chokecherries growing lush in a nearby draw. Lone Moon was good at stripping these tart berries off the branches with her bare fingers. When they got back to camp, they laid many berries in the sun to dry. Lone Moon helped her *ina* and *unci* pound them into dried meat, mixing in tallow to bind them together. Her *ina* would pack this chewy, lightweight *wasna* in rawhide pouches so Sky Eagle, Swift Deer, and Crazy Horse would have ready-to-eat food on their hunts and horse raids.

While women were busy with chokecherries, some men went to the trading post to swap their animal pelts for metal knives, hatchets, tobacco, and things their wives needed. Little girls practiced making small pretend tipis from cottonwood leaves and sticks, and small boys chased each other around, pretending to be warriors. Older boys sat on knolls and watched over the horse herd as they grazed in meadows below.

The sun was high overhead when Lone Moon

heard a commotion. She looked up from beading a moccasin and saw several soldiers approaching the Brule camp. She recognized Lieutenant Grattan as the one her father had pointed out when they rode by Fort Laramie. Twenty-nine soldiers, following the lieutenant, rode three abreast on tall horses. All of them had long rifles attached to their saddles and shiny sabers alongside them. They rode into the camp like they owned it.

Two mules pulled a wagon conveying an enormous black gun with a long barrel. Lone Moon watched several Brule warriors silently mount their horses, string their bows, and encircle family tipis, preparing for a possible attack.

Curiosity momentarily stifled Lone Moon's feelings of fear. She stashed her beading inside the tipi and crept closer for a better view of the soldiers' procession. These men wore blue shirts with shiny yellow buttons and blue pants with a yellow line down the outside of both legs. She noticed their pale, whiskered faces glaring out beneath round, brimmed hats and heard them saying strange words in rough, scratchy voices.

Lt. Grattan shouted something to Conquering Bear, who had walked out to meet the soldiers, but Lone Moon didn't understand the unfamiliar sounding words. Because the lieutenant did not speak Lakota, he had brought a translator. This *ieska* was a white man who obviously couldn't translate or speak the Lakota language very well. Waving a flask of whiskey, slurring his words, and half falling off his horse, he said in a loud, irritating voice, "Lt. Grattan says to hand over the cow who shot the kid, or you'll be shorry. And you bunch of girly warriors get way of our out."

Lone Moon tried to make sense of these mixed-up, odd phrases. Conquering Bear, spokesman for the Brule tribe, said in a calm voice, "I have no authority to turn High Forehead over to you. He is from another tribe. I'm sorry about the cow. The boy had no idea where it came from. He thought it was a stray. I offer you my finest horse in exchange. It is worth much more than a lame cow."

"We're here to take the boy back to the Fort for punishmenting. We're not interestin' in your shtupid, old horse." The drunk interpreter, making many mistakes in the Lakota language, spoke for the lieutenant.

Lone Moon gasped in disbelief. The soldier was disgracing Conquering Bear by sneering at his prized horse. Any warrior would trade four of his own horses to have this magnificent sorrel and white paint. Conquering Bear's face bristled. Mumbling in disgust, he whirled around and strode back toward the council tipi to consult with elders.

Everything happened in an instant. Lone Moon heard some commotion among the soldiers, then a gunshot blasted in her ears. She ran back and dove for cover like a scared jackrabbit, skidding face down near the tipi fire pit. She struggled to her knees, crawled to the door flap, and forced herself to peek out. Her heart felt like oozy mud when she saw Conquering Bear crumpled in a heap on his stomach. Blood squirted out of a gaping hole in his back. He writhed and groaned, gasping for air, then collapsed. Seven warriors immediately surrounded him, their arrows drawn and pointed toward the soldiers. Lone Moon, eyes wild with fright, ducked back inside the tipi and jerked the door flap closed.

"What's going on, Lone Moon? Did I hear a gun shot?" her mother cried from her pallet where she had been napping. "Get down here with me and your *unci!*"

Instead, Lone Moon grabbed her bow, strung an arrow, and pulled it taunt, like Crazy Horse had taught her.

Trying to give herself courage, Lone Moon stammered through lips trembling like vibrating drums, "Protect my *unci* and my *ina*. Be brave. Shoot an arrow into a soldier's heart."

Before her mother could stop her, Lone Moon threw open the door flap, ready to fire. A soldier with a musket aimed directly at her came into focus before her terrified eyes. Her hands shook harder than tipi poles in a fierce wind. Her legs felt as weak and ineffective as winter sun. She hastily launched an arrow; it fizzled harmlessly in front of her. Her mind flashed a question. *Why didn't I practice more like Crazy Horse told me?* Lone Moon jammed her eyes shut, tensed her body, and gritted her teeth. *I hope it doesn't hurt too much when the bullet hits me.* She heard a loud BANG. She felt nothing. Opening her eyelids a slit, she glimpsed the soldier, toppled on his face with a spear protruding from his back. There was a huge hole in front of him where his musket had discharged. Lone Moon saw her father standing over the soldier and realized he had saved her life.

"Stay inside the tipi, girl! Close the flap and keep down!" Sky Eagle shouted as he sprang on his horse and dashed away. Concealing his body by hanging low under his horse's neck, he launched arrows at soldiers, who had dismounted and were shooting back with their long rifles. Galloping between tipis, Lakota warriors showered arrows on the attacking soldiers.

Sobbing and gagging, Lone Moon cowered between her *unci* and *ina* inside the tipi under thick buffalo robes. Her teeth wouldn't quit chattering even though she was hot and sweaty in the suffocating tipi. Putting her hands over her ears to block out the blood-curdling screams, blasting gun shots, squealing horses, and yelping dogs, Lone Moon wept, "Make it stop. Please make it stop. What if my *até* gets killed? What if the baby dies? What if soldiers come inside our tipi and shoot us?"

"You must calm down, little one," comforted Morning Star, holding Lone Moon's trembling body securely in her arms, "your *até* always protects us."

Lt. Grattan was the first soldier to fall, his body covered in arrows. Soldiers trying to discharge their cannon at family tipis were picked off before they could light the fuse. Several soldiers and the drunken interpreter tried running away on foot but were brought down by Brule warriors. Soldiers' horses, frightened by gunshots and clamor, stampeded across the prairie their reins flying free. Lone Moon, nestled inside her mother's buffalo robe, felt a little better, but still worried. Suddenly, there was an abrupt lull. It was almost quiet. The fight was over.

After what seemed like forever, Lone Moon, Yellow Bird, and Morning Star inched outside. Their eyes were immediately assaulted with dead soldiers strewn everywhere, some flopped on their knees, some sprawled out flat, some in a fetal position. Shrieking women ran to help their wounded warriors. The scent of human blood and entrails caught in Lone Moon's nose. The putrid smells made her wretch. This stink was nothing like the unpolluted smell of sacred buffalo blood spilled to provide for the tribe's needs. Tears, like rain on a bare cliff, streamed down her dirty face. She collapsed, dimly aware of Mothers ordering their small children to stay inside the tipis. Other women rushed to help Conquering Bear.

"Get up, child," Yellow Bird insisted. "We must take down the tipi faster than we ever have and load up all our things. We're all moving to a safer place."

"But what about my *ate* and Conquering Bear?" Lone Moon wailed. "Will my *ina* and the baby she is carrying inside her be safe? And how will Crazy Horse find us?"

"Look over there. Your *até* is fine; he is helping wounded men. Your *ina* is assisting medicine men tend to Conquering Bear. They will load Conquering Bear on a pony drag and carry him to our next camp. Morning Star will ride on another pony drag to ease her journey. Crazy Horse always knows where we go and will find us. Hurry and help me before more soldiers come!"

6

CHANGES

BEFORE THE MOON rose, Lone Moon's family and the Brule band left the encampment. Lone Moon was on constant alert. She was terrified soldiers from Fort Laramie would catch them. Her father said the soldiers would stop at nothing to avenge the deaths of Lt. Grattan and his men. Lone Moon rode close to her mother's pony drag all night. When daylight came, she repeatedly scanned the horizon behind them, scared to death of seeing a blue uniform.

As much as everyone hated camping in different spots every night, Lone Moon knew it was safer to keep moving. It took too much time to unload lodge poles and buffalo hide coverings to set up their tipis for one night, so families slept on open prairies with only stars for protection. They ate dried food for breakfast, lunch, and dinner, fearing a campfire might alert soldiers to their whereabouts. Each day, they continued their flight well before dawn. Everyone was exhausted and irritable. *Why isn't Crazy Horse coming to our rescue?* Lone Moon thought. *He must still be on the horse raid.*

Otherwise, he'd be here, she reasoned.

Lone Moon joined with others singing special healing songs and praying for Conquering Bear's recovery. Medicine men tried everything they knew: changing his bandages frequently, applying herbs and salves made from available plants, and bathing his face with cold water. In spite of their efforts, Conquering Bear died nine days after he had been shot.

Lone Moon clasped her arms tightly around her body as she watched the older women preparing Conquering Bear for passing into afterlife. They dressed him in his finest clothes, which included special honoring moccasins with fully beaded soles. They lovingly painted his face red and placed eagle feathers in his hair. Then his body was wrapped in a buffalo robe along with his sacred pipe and personal prayer amulets. His shield, lance, and knife would be tied to the scaffold, which several men built using four straight trees with forked tops. They placed poles on top to support his body. This towering wooden structure was tall enough to raise the corpse closer to the *Creator* and out of reach of any marauding animals.

Lone Moon wiped her runny nose on her sleeve when Conquering Bear's body was lifted onto the scaffold platform. Food was scarce, but his relatives arranged *wasna* and dried turnips beside the chief to provide him nourishment for passage into the spirit world.

Throughout the camp, people mourned Conquering Bear's death. Women wailed and lamented. Some of his male relatives drove sharpened pieces of wood into their legs or arms to express their grief and show their love for him. Some cut their hair short to honor him. Others gave flesh offerings by slicing skin off their legs or arms. Lone Moon looked at her smooth brown arms and wondered if she were brave enough to deface them even for someone she loved.

When Conquering Bear's relatives led his beautiful sorrel and white horse under the scaffold and tied him to one of the poles, Lone Moon prayed the animal would give Conquering Bear's spirit a swift ride on his spiritual journey. Knowing the horse may be shot as part of holy Lakota tradition, she recoiled. She loved this horse and implored the spirits to spare his life. *Instead of being shot, couldn't he be turned loose, so some kind warrior could claim him?* Her whole world seemed to be crumbling. Nothing was right. She longed to ask Crazy Horse why this whole tragedy had happened. *Maybe he could help me understand this madness.*

She walked to a bluff overlooking the river, trying to cope with the wrongness of Conquering Bear's death. "It's not fair. Conquering Bear was only trying to make peace, but the soldiers shot him in the back." Lone Moon shrieked her rage until she was hoarse. Exhausted, she fell on her knees and wept as the sun set in sacred stillness.

The next day, Sky Eagle told his wife in a hushed tone, "We need to leave your Brule relatives today and return to our Oglala camp under the protection of Crazy Horse. I think we will be safer there. Little Thunder has taken over Conquering Bear's leadership and plans to keep this band moving to new locations every night. The scouts informed us that *wasicu's Great White Father* has sent a fierce soldier, General Harney, to find the Brule band and take revenge for the soldiers who were killed. The scouts are saying that Harney detests the Lakota and believes all of us should be obliterated."

Her father's words scared Lone Moon. She did not know what obliterated meant, but it probably wasn't good. She was relieved to be going back to her *tiospaye,* (family unit). She couldn't wait to see Crazy Horse and her *lala* and was glad to not move camp every day.

When Lone Moon's family got back to their Oglala band, Sky Eagle told the community there about Conquering Bear's death. Mourning and weeping began again. *In normal times, our return would have been greeted with feasting and celebration,* Lone Moon noted with sadness.

Shortly after helping her mother and grandmother set up their tipi, Lone Moon saw a cloud of dust rising on the horizon. Her shoulders contracted in immediate panic, afraid it was soldiers. Then she heard cheering and realized Crazy Horse, his warriors, and Swift Deer were returning from their horse raid. At least eighty horses thundered into a large rope corral in the meadow. Blacks, bays, sorrels, paints, and greys snorted and whinnied, searching for ways to escape. When they noticed a stream flowing through the corral, the horses settled down, drank thirstily, and started devouring the abundant green grass, soon forgetting their long excursion.

Crazy Horse slid off his tired horse with a triumphant grin but gave Lone Moon a questioning look, puzzled at the pervading somber mood. Lone Moon forced a big smile, but she knew he could detect deep sadness behind it. The people were happy to see the new horses, yet everyone was glum and restrained.

The elders immediately called Crazy Horse and his warriors into council. Lone Moon could see the scene in her mind. *Elders relating the heartbreaking news of Conquering Bear's death and sordid details of how Lt. Grattan and his soldiers had attacked the Brule camp. Crazy Horse grieving and trying to control his anger. He'll probably have to leave right away to save his relatives' band.*

Crazy Horse strode out of the council tipi. Seeing Lone Moon, he asked her to grab him a fresh horse and some *wasna* to eat on the way.

"But you barely got back. I don't want you to leave again so soon," Lone Moon brooded, biting hard on the end of one braid.

"Lone Moon, you know we have to help Little Thunder. He might be in big trouble. We must think what's best for all people, not merely ourselves. Jump on Cloud and ride with me for a little way."

38

Lone Moon rode with him to the trees. Tears she meant to keep in leaked out and made little stains down the front of her dress. Crazy Horse rode alongside, trying to comfort her. "These are tough times and very hard to understand, but we will get through them together. I'll be back as soon as I can. We can talk more then."

Lone Moon nodded, but her heart felt as heavy as a bag of mud. She turned her back and reined Cloud toward camp. She did not want to watch Crazy Horse ride away.

➤➤7◄◄

IN TROUBLE

OTHER TROUBLES SOON took Lone Moon's mind off Crazy Horse. Her grandfather was not happy. He had heard about Lone Moon's actions during Grattan's attack of the Brule camp. Even though he didn't take any pleasure in doing so, it was his duty to reprimand his granddaughter.

Swift Deer's usual jovial face appeared weary and distressed. Deep wrinkles slashed his forehead, his errant eyebrows puckered over squinted eyes, and his lips pressed hard together like cracks in a rock.

"What were you thinking, Lone Moon, trying to shoot a white soldier?" her grandfather said in a stern voice that Lone Moon had never heard him use before. "You put yourself, your mother, and your grandmother in grave danger. You must learn to think before you act. Hand me your bow and arrows. From now on, you behave like a girl and put aside boyish ways. Your grandmother will teach you to be a proper Lakota woman, who helps all our people by knowing who you are and what your responsibilities are to our *tiospaye*. We all need to do the best we can to help each other in these trying times."

Lone Moon fixed her wispy, dark eyelashes on his moccasins. It was disrespectful to look at her grandfather while he was scolding her. She didn't dare answer back or try to defend herself. That would be against Lakota ways. Swift Deer gave her a compassionate look as he walked away, but she could tell he was disappointed in her actions.

Lone Moon's insides felt like they were being stuffed through a knothole. She was ashamed to have disappointed her *lala*. And she wanted to explain that she was trying to protect her *ina*, the baby, and her *unci*. *Girls are powerless. They aren't allowed to fight soldiers or go to war.*

"And now, I don't even have a bow," she muttered to herself.

Lone Moon dragged the toes of her moccasins through powdery dirt back to her tipi. Twisting her mouth in resigned acceptance, she shouldered the role of obeying her elders. *I will learn to be a good Lakota woman. I'll try not to gag when I must soften buffalo hides with slimy brains or complain about taking time to bead in neat, straight rows, or...*

Fancy Moccasins strutted in front of her, interrupting her thoughts.

Oh no, not the young braves. They always show up at my worst times and probably have something rude to say.

"Why such a sad face, warrior woman?" Fancy Moccasins jeered. "I guess Crazy Horse didn't

41

teach you to shoot so good."

"Were you scared out of your wits when you saw the ugly white soldier? Next time, you should leave fighting to men like us," added Rattling Leaf.

Lone Moon tried to ignore them, but their insults scorched her brain.

"Yah, stick to playing with your dolls. I think I'll start calling you Crazy Moon." Fancy Moccasins guffawed at his own joke.

Rattling Leaf laughed with him. "Or what about Limp Arrow? Ha, ha, ha."

"I wish you'd both fall off a cliff," she growled through clenched teeth. She shot daggers at them through narrowed eyes before bolting inside her tipi. She kicked the doll she had made for the baby off her buffalo hide bedding. It landed clear across the tipi.

⬤➤➤ 8 ◀◀⬤

MORE TRAGEDY

IF I WERE a boy, I would ride with Crazy Horse. I would follow him into battle and count coup on wasicu. Counting coup is the bravest deed a warrior can accomplish. I would touch the enemy without being harmed. Crazy Horse is so daring and quick, he has counted coup more than all other warriors.

She imagined herself as a warrior. In her daydream, she had a red hawk feather tied in her hair, knowing the hawk's spirit would provide her swiftness and endurance like it did for Crazy Horse. She sneaked up on a *wasicu*, hung off to one side of her pony to seem invisible, and then suddenly sat up straight. She whapped the enemy with her coup stick, then galloped off in a cover of dust before the person realized what had happened. She saw herself riding into camp and proudly receiving an eagle feather for her bravery and boldness.

Morning Star entered the tipi, jarring Lone Moon back to the present.

"You've had a rough day," her mother said, reaching down to rub Lone Moon's back in empathy. "Growing up is not easy in these chaotic times, but your family is here to help you through it. I can't promise things will ever be like they were before the *wasicu* came, but we'll find ways to survive. And there will be more happy times."

The sun rose and set three times before she saw Crazy Horse approaching. His shoulders were slumped and his head was down. She ran to meet him, but he didn't seem to notice her. When he was inside the circle of tipis, he slipped off his horse and crumpled to his knees. Lone Moon noticed his wet, dull eyes. People burst from their tipis and gathered close around Crazy Horse to hear his report. Worry creased their faces. Lone Moon could barely hear Crazy Horse's broken, grated whisper.

"Slaughtered in their sleep on the Creek of Blue Waters," he rasped in halting words. "Little Thunder's band...didn't have a chance...dead bodies lying everywhere, even little children and women...scalps taken...bodies hacked...tipis ripped apart or burned...horses stolen."

Crazy Horse pounded the earth in anger and exasperation. Barely able to speak, he continued his horrible story, "A woman, who managed to hide, saw soldiers loading buffalo hides, guns, and food onto their horses. She said General Harney was laughing and congratulating his men on their surprise early morning attack." Crazy Horse hiccupped back a sob. "... It wasn't an attack; it was a cowardly massacre." He paused, closed his eyes and shook his head in disbelief. "Then...as the soldiers rode off," Crazy Horse's voice cracked in anguish, "the woman said Harney raised his rifle and shouted, 'This will show those savages for what they did to Lt. Grattan and his men.' I took the woman back to her relatives in Spotted Tail's camp." Crazy Horse's chest caved in grief. He put his hands over his haggard face as if to block the hideous memories of all he'd seen. No one spoke, each trying to grasp the horror of this absurd massacre.

Lone Moon staggered away, needing to be alone. Her brain was on fire with contorted thoughts. *The Brule warriors had been defending their women and children when Lt. Grattan and his men attacked them over that witless cow. But Harney and his soldiers had brutally struck down the Brule people while they were sleeping.*

"I don't understand, I'll never understand the *wasicu*," she yelled angrily into gullies and surrounding silent hills. *Wasicu...wasicu...* echoed back to her. She shivered, unable to stop an icy waterfall of fear cascading down her spine.

For several sleeps, people grieved, going without food to honor their Brule friends. During this time, Morning Star cut the tip off one finger and stayed away from camp for a while, mourning her lost relatives. Lone Moon thanked her father for insisting his family move back to the Oglala camp instead of staying with Little Thunder. Otherwise, they may not be alive.

Later, the council met with Crazy Horse to

discuss their options. Lone Moon sneaked up beside the council tipi to listen, knowing it was wrong to eavesdrop. *I simply need to know what they decide,* she justified to herself.

Younger warriors expressed their fury and wanted to leave immediately to find and kill Harney and his troops before they could return to a fort. Older warriors thought it was best to relocate and prepare for upcoming cold weather. Crazy Horse understood the youthful warriors' plea for revenge, but cautioned them about needing to provide food and shelter for their families.

"The buffalo may be very scarce and difficult to find this year. Without them, we won't survive winter," Lone Moon overheard Crazy Horse tell the council.

"Buffalo are bothered by the *wasicu* and his *Holy Trail* just like we are." said He Dog.

"Wagon train horses, mules, and oxen eat all the grass for four spear throws on both sides of the trail and trample what they don't eat," High Back Bone added. "No wonder the buffalo have moved on."

"White hunters shoot our buffalo and only take their hides and tongues," said Worm, Crazy Horse's father. "The rest of our sacred animal is left to rot or for buzzards and wolves to feast on."

"And they throw away empty bags, broken wheels, old clothes, rotten food, and other junk all along the trail," complained Hump.

"We need to go to Powder River country to see if any buffalo are still there." He Dog said.

The men finally agreed it was imperative to move and find buffalo, or face starvation in the freezing moons ahead. They would have to wait to avenge the Brule deaths.

"We better send scouts out to find buffalo tomorrow," Crazy Horse advised, his voice sounding urgent. "We have no time to waste."

9

THE SURPRISE

BABIES CRYING, DOGS yipping, women gossiping, men talking, and kids laughing as they chased each other around. Lone Moon needed to leave this noisy place and try to make sense of all that had happened lately. She jumped on her pony, Cloud, and whistled for her dog, Arrow, to follow. Going out alone on the wide, open prairie felt like having a cool, refreshing drink of water. She galloped away, with her muscular legs clinging to Cloud's belly and her coal-black braids flying straight back from her face. Pausing on a rocky hillside dotted with a few pine trees, she slid down from Cloud's slick back and allowed him free rein to graze on sparse grass. Lone Moon sat on a soft clump of buffalo grass. Arrow squirmed into her lap, licking her face, as if trying to make her feel better. She petted the top of his shaggy head, massaged his flea-bitten ears, and carefully pulled sharp needle grass and cockle burrs from the long hair on his legs and belly. Cloud wandered over and put his muzzle on Lone Moon's shoulder. She reached up and scratched his long nose.

"How do dogs and ponies always seem to know when a person needs love and understanding?" she questioned aloud, smiling at them.

She laid back on spongy pine needles, Arrow snuggled beside her. So many things were changing and clashing in her world. She delighted in quiet prairies and round-topped buttes where things didn't seem to change. A soft wind caressed her face and calmed her thoughts. Scraggly sagebrush hid the prickly pear cactus, so predators had a difficult time uncovering a meadowlark's nest hidden in dry grass underneath. A safe distance away, the yellow-breasted bird sang its joy. Fluffy clouds moseyed across a deep blue sky. Everything seemed peaceful.

Why can't we live in peace with the wasicu? She wondered. *Where do all the soldiers come from? Why don't they like us? Why do they want to chase us off this land or move us to places called reservations? Crazy Horse says this land does not belong to anyone; we belong to it. My heart tells me to love all people, including wasicu. But my mind tells me to fear white soldiers.*

Shaking her head in frustration, Lone Moon climbed on Cloud and loped across the sage-filled plains. In a deep gully, she splashed cool, creek water on her face and drank deeply before allowing Cloud to get a drink. She plucked some sweetgrass growing nearby and braided it to take home to her *unci,* who lit a dried sweetgrass braid before every meal. Lone Moon pictured Yellow Bird turning and fanning smoke into each of the four sacred directions, while saying a prayer. To the east she prayed for truth, peace, and new life, to the south for compassion, warmth, and generosity, to the west for wisdom, patience, and good health, and to the north for strength, protection, and understanding. It was soothing to listen to her sing-songy tone when she recited these daily prayers.

Lone Moon made Cloud walk to camp, checking his attempt of racing to the other horses. She breathed in the clean smell of sage and heard birds warbling love songs to each other. Lone Moon felt serene, and she resolved to be a better helper to her *unci*. Her *lala* taught her to look for good in all creatures; she would try to see good in the *wasicu*. Swift Deer was full of wisdom. He said all creatures were one with each other, all inhabiting Mother Earth, all breathing the same air, all warming in the same sun, all dependent on each other. He often said, "*Mitakuye Oyas'in* (we are all relatives); we are all related, not solely to other humans but to all creatures on earth, including non-living things like rocks. Everyone and everything have a purpose in life."

Lone Moon turned Cloud loose in the horse pasture after rubbing him down with a handful of sage. She found a piece of dried meat to give Arrow, who thanked her by wagging his tail and wriggling against her leg. She slogged home, knowing she would be expected to help pack things for moving further north to seek buffalo. But as she rounded the corner of the tipi, her heart caught in her throat. Tied to a hitching post was the most amazing yearling horse she'd ever seen. This filly was dark bay with a black mane and tail. Lightning bolt shapes decorated both of her sleek sides. She had three white stockings that reached to her hocks and a light patch over one eye that trickled down to her muzzle.

Crazy Horse sauntered up beside the filly, grinning like a mischievous child. "Do you like her?"

"Oh Cousin, is she really mine?" Lone Moon clasped both her fists in front of her mouth and raised her eyebrows as high as they could go. Her ebony eyes flickered in excitement.

"From head to tail, she's all yours."

"She's... she's absolutely beautiful! Thank you so much. I've wanted a new horse forever, and this one is perfect."

Lone Moon walked slowly to the little horse, talking in a low tone as she extended her open hand. The filly threw her head up, snorted, and pulled back on the lead rope. Her eyes gleamed large and suspicious. Lone Moon stood quietly, murmuring reassuring words.

"It's okay, little girl. I won't hurt you. We're going to be great friends."

Curiosity overcoming her fear, the filly put her head down and sniffed at Lone Moon's hand, blowing little snorts of air through her nostrils.

"That's right, sweet girl, smell my hand. You can trust me."

Lone Moon eased one finger closer and stroked her muzzle. She breathed into the filly's nostrils, joining spirits with the little horse, who looked wary but didn't try to pull away. Lone Moon knew it would take a while before the filly would show enough trust to allow her ears and neck to be petted. But she made a vow to work with the young horse every day and gain her confidence.

Lone Moon stepped back, pursed her lips, cocked her head to one side, curled her forefinger and thumb under her chin, gazing at the filly as she pondered.

"I think I'll call her... Magpie."

"That fits her," approved Crazy Horse. "She does have same colorings of that bird. I'll take her back to the corral, but remember she is your responsibility now, and you must protect and treat her well. Now, you go help your *unci* with dinner, or we will both be in trouble."

Lone Moon skipped into the family tipi, chattering like a magpie, telling her *ina* and *unci* all about the surprise filly.

"You were right *Ina* when you said there would be happy times." Lone Moon smiled.

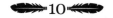

TATANKA

HE DOG WAS a long way off when Lone Moon heard his shouts, "TATANKA, *TATANKA*, **TATANKA, BUFFALO!**" He streaked into camp, pulled his lather-soaked horse to a sliding stop, and jumped off.

Gasping for air he managed to huff out, "More buffalo ... than trees in the forests! Plenty to supply us ...for...for...whole winter. Only two campsites away ... big grassy plain!"

People mobilized faster than a stirred ant pile, knowing the buffalo may relocate any time. Little girls danced with excitement, and little boys chased each other, pretending to either be a hunter or a buffalo. Lone Moon, who had been training Magpie, hurried the filly back to the horse corrals. She busied herself helping Yellow Bird assemble scraping tools and fill bladder bags with creek water. Morning Star loaded their pony drag with elk bone fleshers to skin hides off slain buffalo, sharp knives and axes for cutting meat, and rawhide bags to protect organs and brains. Lone Moon positioned full bladder bags on the drag so her mother could strap them down to prevent spilling.

Everyone had a role in the hunt. They laughed and joked while scurrying around. Wives mixed paint for their husbands' faces and bodies. Warriors said prayers as they applied the paint to ensure a safe, successful hunt. Young braves caught trained buffalo-running horses and brought them to hunters so they could paint their sides and necks. Medicine men prayed for the hunters' protection and offered special thanks to buffalo spirits for giving their lives so the tribe could survive. Older men sharpened tools for gutting and quartering huge bison and loaded additional weapons onto pony drags to replace any warriors might lose during the hectic chase. Hunters strapped extra arrows, knives, and spears onto their horses. They had decorated their arrows with a special mark, so the wives could tell which buffalo they shot.

The *akicita,* men elected by the council to oversee the hunt, told four young warriors, "We have selected you to feed the elderly and widows among us who have no one to bring them buffalo. Today you will hunt for them."

The young men smiled to have been chosen for this great honor of fulfilling Lakota tradition that ensured everyone got a fair share of meat and hides.

Lone Moon fluttered about like a butterfly. She knew the importance of this hunt, not only for meat, but for buffalo robes, bedding, and tipi coverings.

Buffalo rawhide would be used for ropes, bridles, containers, and shields; bones would become tools, utensils, war clubs, and whistles; bladders would serve as bags for carrying water; sinew for sewing thread; horns for arrow points and decorations; even blood would be boiled down for pudding. Buffalo provided almost everything they needed to live. Lone Moon had listened to elders telling stories from days long ago about vast herds of bison that stretched from horizon to horizon, blanketing the prairie. Dust their hooves stirred darkened the sky, and Mother Earth would shake and rumble when buffalo stampeded. But when the *wasicu* wagon trains arrived, buffalo had scattered, and large herds were difficult to find.

Lone Moon leaned against a pony drag and let her mind wander. *I wish I could be involved in this frenzy, chaos, and danger.* In her imaginary world, she pressed Cloud into an exploding gallop, dashed after the bulky animals, rode dangerously close to a big bull, and struck him with the flat of her hand, then rode back to the crowd. She could almost hear cheers of amazement for her counting coup on a buffalo.

Lone Moon knew in real life all the females would watch from a safe distance, waiting for one of their men to kill a buffalo. Women would then unsheathe their razor-sharp knives and fleshers, skin the buffalo, and slice the meat into manageable slabs for loading onto pony drags. Considering the hard work involved in these tasks and in tanning hides,

Lone Moon thought, *Boys have more fun. After the first frantic chase, they get to take fresh horses to hunters and ride close to buffalo. Now, that would be exciting.* A tiny idea stirred in her head.

Morning Star scolded, "Lone Moon, quit daydreaming and get busy. We have much to do and little time."

When all was ready, Lone Moon mounted Cloud and waited to take part in the procession to the hunting grounds. The *akicita* led a colorful parade of people on horseback. Next, came hunters, with their faces painted in spiritual, protective designs and mounted on their vibrant horses. Envious young braves, wishing they could hunt, rode and led extra horses and followed behind the hunters. Elderly men, who were gesturing with both arms in the air and bragging about how much better things were in days of old, intermingled with these boys. Lone Moon slipped in line with the older girls, riding their own horses. Women, draped in bright yellow and red blankets, trailed behind the girls, guiding their pony drag horses. Smaller children rode on the drags, bumping along beside tools and weapons.

Everyone was chattering with expectancy but knew to be quiet as they rode into a valley close to the buffalo herd. Lone Moon watched the *akicita*, Crazy Horse, and a few other warriors snake through scrub cedar to get a better view. Taking caution not to be seen, the scouting group peered over the crest onto a flat plain filled with black, shaggy beasts, who were milling around totally unaware of the impending hunt. Some buffalo grazed complacently on tall prairie grass, with magpies balanced on their shaggy backs plucking fleas. Cows took dirt baths in powdery wallows, young bulls jostled each other with their emerging horns while older bulls grunted their impatience.

Hunters had their spears, guns, bows, and arrows ready, watching for the signal to begin. When Crazy Horse silently raised his elk horn quirt above his head, the hunters, bursting with energy, charged the surprised buffalo. Women, old men, and children scrambled up a hill away from any danger to observe the drama unfold.

Startled buffalo stampeded away, but the warriors outsmarted them by singling groups of the huge animals off the main herd. Hunters rode fearlessly into these smaller bunches. Sounds of arrows and spears whizzing, men yelling, horses galloping, and buffalo grunting, crammed the aborted silence. Dust from the horse and buffalo hooves cutting into dry soil clogged the air and shrouded the view. Lone Moon, squinting her eyes, soon spotted dead buffalo lying on the ground with men standing over them. Invigorated by success, hunters swung onto fresh, lively horses and sped after the main herd to make another rush on them. Women dashed out to start processing meat.

With their eyes glued on the rolling action, Morning Star and Yellow Bird waited for Sky Eagle to shoot a buffalo. Lone Moon sighted some stragglers from the buffalo herd. These young buffalo drifted around in circles, as if confused about what had happened and unsure where to go. Lone Moon recognized her chance.

No one noticed her sneak over to Cloud and shinny onto his back. Without thinking, Lone Moon kicked Cloud's sides hard with both feet, urging him into a full run. She ignored warning shouts from behind her and charged into a group of five buffalo. Hot blood hammered in her ears once she understood her peril. *I didn't realize how large these young bulls are.*

Cloud, as he had been trained, crowded against one beast pushing it away from the others. A familiar gamey smell of buffalo hair infiltrated Lone Moon's nostrils. Dust smarted in her eyes. Her heart seemed to stop beating. She leaned way over Cloud, clutching his mane in one hand and stretching her other arm to its limit. *I'm only three fingers away from touching its backbone and counting coup. I will connect with its spirit!*

With no warning, the agile, young bull lowered his head, pivoted, and charged directly at her. Instinctively, Cloud threw his head straight up and twisted aside to avoid the assault. Lone Moon's sweaty hands tried to cling to Cloud's mane, but she had leaned too far and teetered off balance. She dug her heels into his slippery shoulders, but the force of Cloud's contortions jarred her loose, wrenched her from the horse's back, and slammed her into dry, baked earth with a hard thud.

Flickering stars encircled her head. A sour sickness invaded her stomach. Her heartbeat sounded like a thunderous drum. Coughing dirt, spitting broken bits of scratchy sage brush, and gasping for breath, Lone Moon unwittingly rolled into a patch of spiny prickly pear cactus.

The young buffalo bull wheeled around, lurched to a stop, and pawed the ground in anger. Lone Moon could smell fury on its breath. She tried to scramble away, terrified the powerful bull would ram his shaggy, horned head into her body. She was entangled in cactus and sagebrush and couldn't move. She raised a limp arm to protect her face. *I'll never see my ina again or the new baby,* flashed through her brain.

Suddenly she felt herself being swooped up. *Is it over? Is this how it feels to fly to the spirit world?*

"You could have been killed! You reckless girl," Crazy Horse scolded, stuffing her dazed body behind him on his horse. She was crossways with her head hanging over one side and her legs on the other. She grasped onto Crazy Horse's waist to keep from falling off.

Spurred into a high lope, his horse easily outdistanced the astonished buffalo. Crazy Horse dropped Lone Moon at her mother's feet. "I hope she's learned a lesson," He said in a brusque voice. Through her pain and embarrassment, Lone Moon watched as he galloped away to rejoin the hunt and heard him holler over his shoulder, "Thank the spirits you're alive."

59

⟫⟫11⟪⟪

BARBS

L ONE MOON'S BACK, arms, legs, and face felt like a thousand hornets had stung her. She tried pulling some cactus spines out, but they cut into her fingers and made them bleed. Her muscles shouted in pain whenever she moved, and her head throbbed worse than a smashed finger.

"Sit still, Lone Moon, I can't get them out if you are fidgeting," her *unci* said, plucking cactus spines out one by one.

"But it really hurts, *Unci*. You pinch my skin so hard," Lone Moon whimpered. "My arms feel like they're on fire."

"I know, little one, it's pure agony, but if I don't get them all out, they will get infected. Bite on this stick. I must dig this deep one out with the end of my knife blade."

"OUCH!" Lone Moon clamped down on the stick, squeezed her arm tight, and held her breath.

When all the barbs were finally wrenched from her skin, Morning Star took Lone Moon to a beaver pond and gently rubbed cool, soft mud all over her body. As the mud dried, her soreness and stinginess lessened.

"Oh, that feels so much better," Lone Moon said.

"Now let's both go swimming and wash this mud off. I think I have as much on me as you do," Morning Star laughed.

They soaked in cool water until Lone Moon's toes and fingers shriveled. After getting dressed, they walked hand-in-hand back to the tipi.

"I'll start supper while you sit in the sun and get warm," said Morning Star.

Two gangly young braves came ambling by. Fancy Moccasins pointed at Lone Moon and laughed. "Did Crazy Horse teach you how to tumble off your horse into cactus, little brave buffalo hunter?"

"Be quiet! You don't know anything. Crazy Horse saved my life." Lone Moon snapped, her eyes tightening into angry slits.

"I bet the buffalo were so frightened by these long braids," teased Rattling Leaf as he yanked on one. The boys swaggered away chuckling loudly, shoving each other down, and yelping as they pretended to be Lone Moon rolling in cactus.

Lone Moon's face burned. *What can I do to get back at those awful boys?*

"I hope a skunk sprays you right in the face," Lone Moon yelled at their backs. She grabbed a dry clod and threw it at them, then winced from darts of pain the throwing caused.

"Oh, don't get so upset, Lone Moon. They're only teasing you because they like you," said Morning

Star, overhearing the ruckus.

"Well, I don't like their teasing. I think they're mean," Lone Moon pouted. "What else can go wrong today?"

Later that afternoon, her uncle, Bear Claw, came over to their tipi and reprimanded Lone Moon. "You and your pony could have been gored by that buffalo. You acted very irresponsibly, only thinking of yourself. Your *ina* and *unci* love you, but they have spent so much time tending to your cactus punctures, they've barely had time to preserve the family's share of buffalo meat. They have been generous with their time for you, now it's your turn to be generous and help them tan hides. When you do things for others, it takes your mind off your own hurts and problems. And remember, always be grateful for good people and good things in your life."

Lone Moon limped away with her head down, chewing the end of one braid. She knew her uncle was right. She had been foolish. *If Crazy Horse hadn't been nearby, I could have been killed. And poor Cloud, he might have been hurt because of my dumb idea. When will I learn to think things through?*

Her *até*, Sky Eagle, didn't say a word. Fathers and Mothers didn't discipline their own children; discipline and guidance were left to grandfathers, uncles, grandmothers, and aunts. The parents' role was to love and cherish their precious children, teaching them by example. Her *até* hunted to provide food, protected their family, and accompanied Crazy Horse on excursions that helped everyone. Her *ina* cooked, gathered wild food, tanned hides, processed food, sewed and decorated clothes and moccasins. She also took down and set up their tipi whenever the band moved to a new location.

The next day, Lone Moon's arms and fingers were aching from scraping a buffalo hide with an old elk horn. She couldn't stop gagging at the smell of slimy brains every time she had to smear more on the hide to keep it moist. Crazy Horse slipped up behind her. He sat down next to her in silence for a long while. Lone Moon was afraid to look at him.

He cleared his throat, paused, then said in a soft, kind voice, "An instant later and you would have been dead. Imagine the grief that would have caused your family and me. Everyone makes bad choices at times, but wise ones learn from their mistakes. Make sure you learn from this."

Lone Moon's eyes filled with tears, but strangely she felt better. She appreciated how Crazy Horse could criticize her but still be nice, and he didn't say a lot of useless words. She continued scraping the hide, but it didn't seem so difficult now with him beside her.

12

EARLY FLOWER

L ONE MOON WAS rubbing sleep from her eyes
a few days later when Morning Star said, "A
family from Sitting Bull's band joined our camp.
They have relatives here and want to be under
Crazy Horse's protection. They are setting up their
tipi next to ours."

Lone Moon peeked from inside her tipi door flap
and watched while the Mother set up a tipi. A girl
about Lone Moon's size wandered out to help her
mother place four heavy buffalo skin coverings
over tall tipi poles. Lone Moon's eye's opened with
interest. *Maybe she would be my friend; I've never
had a girl friend my age.*

"Let's go over and welcome them, Lone Moon.
Bring some of those plums you picked yesterday.
Grandmother, will you make extra buffalo stew so
we can invite them for supper? They must be tired
after their long journey."

Morning Star took Lone Moon's hand and led her
to their new neighbor's tipi. "*Mas'ke* (hello) and
welcome to our camp. I'm Morning Star, and this

64

is my daughter, Lone Moon."

The Mother stopped what she was doing and stepped forward. *"Mas'ke,* it's nice to meet you both." Then easing her daughter in front of her, she said, "This is Early Flower, and my name is Crow Wing."

While their mothers chatted, each girl stared at the other, unsure of what to say or do. Lone Moon thought, *I like her wavy, brownish-black hair and how the ends of her braids curl like buffalo grass. She's kind of skinny, but very pretty.*

Early Flower noticed how Lone Moon's dark braids, tied with rawhide strings, were crooked and unruly. *She looks adventurous and fun,* Early Flower thought.

Prompted by her mother, Early Flower politely asked, "Lone Moon would you like to see a doll I made?"

She rummaged through their pony drag and brought out a doll similar to the one Lone Moon had made for the new baby. Lone Moon noticed it didn't have a face either.

"That's really nice. Your stitches are so tiny and neat," Lone Moon complimented. "If you like, I can show you around camp, and we can play by the sandy creek bank."

Soon, the girls were chattering like prairie dogs and became fast friends despite their personalities being quite different. Early Flower shook her head when Lone Moon splashed right through the deep mud puddles, not caring if her moccasins got stained. Lone Moon rolled her eyes whenever Early Flower went out of her way to avoid a mud puddle to keep her own moccasins clean. Lone Moon acted as impetuous as a hungry bear, but Early Flower was as patient as a cat waiting to catch a bird. Rarely out of each other's sight after their first meeting, they laughed and giggled over many trivial things. Lone Moon gave Early Flower some pretty rocks from her collection and shared her most private secrets with this new friend. Early Flower gifted Lone Moon with a small jingle bell her father had gotten at the trading post. With Early Flower's help, Lone Moon didn't mind the onerous chore of picking up dried buffalo dung for cook fires. They made a game of it, seeing who could stack the dry, crusty, round plops into the highest pile before they toppled over.

"Be careful around those thorny bushes. We don't want our bags to snag on them and burst open," Lone Moon warned her new friend on a hot afternoon.

She and Early Flower carried buffalo bladder bags full of cool creek water. The heavy, jiggling bags sloshed water on their moccasins.

Suddenly, Fancy Moccasins and Rattling Leaf jumped from behind some trees and poked at the brimming bags with sharpened sticks.

"Wouldn't it be sad if these sticks broke open your bags," they teased. "You'd really be in trouble then."

"Don't you dare!" Lone Moon warned, planting

her feet. "Our *inas* are waiting for this water."

Fancy Moccasins pulled a green grass snake from behind his back and stuck it in the girls' faces. They both shrieked and ran toward camp, jostling the fragile bags in front of them. The laughing boys chased after them with the wriggly snake. Early Flower, barreling in fright down the uneven trail, lost one of her moccasins. Rattling Leaf grabbed it and threw it into a tall oak tree. Crazy Horse was sitting on a rock near the camp sharpening some arrows. When the boys spotted him, they skedaddled like startled wild turkeys.

"Fancy Moccasins and Rattling Leaf are worse than fifty mosquito bites. All they do is bother us," Lone Moon complained, rubbing her brow in aggravation. Crazy Horse merely smiled, remembering pranks he had pulled in his youth.

"Those boys make me so angry," Lone Moon said to Early Flower as they walked to their tipis.

"I agree, and how am I supposed to get my moccasin back?"

"Don't worry, Crazy Horse has probably already climbed the tree to fetch it." Then wrinkling her nose in determination, Lone Moon added, "We need to find a way to get even with those boys."

67

◀▬13▬▶

GETTING EVEN

R ELAXING BY THE creek one day fishing for
blue gills, Lone Moon suddenly twisted her
mouth sideways and peered at Early Flower with
a devious look.

"What are you plotting?" Early Flower asked.

"Maybe we could trick those irritating boys," Lone
Moon mused, chewing on her thumbnail. Lone
Moon bounced on her tiptoes while explaining her
plan for getting back at the boys.

"You'll have to snitch some white paint from
your *ina's* bag," Lone Moon said gleefully clapping
her fists together. "I know where I can get a long
rawhide string and some white trading post
blankets."

Early Flower, drawing her eyebrows into a
dubious frown said, "I'm not sure about this idea.
It sounds dangerous and crazy. What if we get
caught?"

"I know how to creep like scouts do. We won't get
caught," Lone Moon reassured her.

Early Flower shrugged, knowing it wouldn't do

any good to try to change Lone Moon's mind.

That night when a half moon was high in the sky, Lone Moon, carrying two white blankets and rawhide string, scratched the side of the tipi where Early Flower slept. Almost instantly, Early Flower slipped through her door flap without making a sound and crawled to where Lone Moon was hiding. Careful not to alert sleeping dogs or night scouts watching from their vantage point above the camp, they crept from bush to bush to the southwest end of the rope horse corral. Fancy Moccasins and Rattling Leaf were on night duty watching above the corral's north end. A pale moon snaked in and out of the thin clouds. The girls could hear the boys bragging about how brave they were.

"I bet I could capture more horses than Crazy Horse."

"That's nothing, I could shoot down a buffalo with one arrow."

Lone Moon thrust one end of the rawhide string at Early Flower, "Tie this right under the lariat rope that keeps horses from getting out of the corral."

An owl hooted; a horse snorted. Early Flower jumped, fear crisscrossing her face.

"Let's get out of here while we still can!" Early Flower stammered in a hushed voice.

"Oh, it was nothing," Lone Moon whispered, trying not to show her own concern. "We can't quit now. We've almost got it. Hurry up. Tie your end tight. I'll be back before you know it."

"What, you're leaving me here alone?"

"You know that's our plan. Now, don't make a sound."

Lone Moon slithered across grass to a tree on the corral's southeast side and anchored her end of the string with three secure knots about one moccasin foot off the ground. Her fingers worked fast and sure. She noted with satisfaction a big patch of prickly pear cactus growing on the other side of their taut trap. She crawled on her belly back toward Early Flower, stopping often to peek and listen for the boys to notice anything unusual. The horses, providing a shield, watched her progress with their puzzled ears pointed ahead, but they didn't give her away. Sweat trickled off her face. Fancy Moccasins and Rattling Leaf were lying on their backs gazing at stars and still boasting about future brave deeds. Engrossed in their conversation, they were unaware anything was going on below them. Lone Moon couldn't believe they didn't hear her heart banging in double drumbeats. Early Flower breathed a sigh of relief when Lone Moon came near. Lone Moon swiftly retrieved their bag from the bushes. Taking out white gooey paint, she smeared it all over her face and hands and motioned for Early Flower to do likewise. Early Flower frowned, but she applied the paint, protest still festering in her eyes. Lone Moon unfolded two white blankets and handed one to Early Flower, who clutched it to her trembling body. Lone Moon reached for the tail end of the lariat rope slipknot that secured the corral and kept horses inside. Her whole body strained with nervousness. She eased the rope loose bit by bit until it dropped silently without any horses noticing. Putting her forefinger on her lips, she gestured for Early Flower to follow her. Lone Moon scuttled around the rope fence perimeter to the corral's northwest corner. On a silent count of three fingers, she and Early Flower leaped up flapping white blankets while making screechy, ghostly sounds. White paint on their faces glowed eerily in the moonlight. Startled horses stampeded toward the south end of the corral. Finding the rope gate open, they charged outside. They easily jumped over the cactus patch before galloping off into the night, snorting, bucking, and squealing.

Tiny rocks flew as the terrified boys scrambled to their feet, eyes as big as bowls, not believing what they were seeing in the corral.

"Ghosts!"

"Demons!"

"Evil Spirits!"

They shrieked, hopping on their toes and waving their arms back and forth. Stumbling about, not sure what to do first, it finally dawned on them to sprint after the horses through the opening in the rope fence, as Lone Moon hoped they would.

STUMBLE! CRASH! SNAP! They tripped over the rawhide string trap, which somersaulted them into needle-like spines of the cactus bed. The words that sailed back were not nice ones.

The whole camp awakened and people ran in every direction, trying to figure out what was causing all the commotion. Screaming women and children spewed from their tipis and huddled together for protection. Dogs yapped and snarled at an invisible enemy. Men grabbed their bows and arrows. Some women and elders ran for safety in the trees.

"What's going on?"

"Is it a Crow horse raid?"

"A mountain lion?"

"White soldiers?"

They shouted to each other, unmasked fear in their voices.

Lone Moon and Early Flower scurried to hide behind some bushes, hands over their mouths to suppress laughter. They stuffed blankets into their bag and covered it with dead leaves.

Instantly, the camp's alert plan was put into motion. Several warriors jumped on ponies they always kept tethered by their tipis for emergencies and rode off to wrangle the horses back to the corral's safety. Other warriors got ready for an attack. People scanned the horizon for any unusual movements. Lone Moon and Early Flower rushed to the creek and washed white paint off their faces. They slipped back into the chaos of panicked people, pretending to have just awakened.

Soon warriors returned with the runaway herd and secured them inside the fence. Everyone calmed down and returned to their beds.

Back in her tipi, lying on her soft buffalo blanket, Lone Moon couldn't stifle a giggle as she recalled the boy's petrified reaction when they saw the "white ghosts." She couldn't wait to tell Crazy Horse all about their comical stunt. But somewhere in her mind, Crazy Horse's voice spoke, "Without horses, the Lakota would be easily defeated. It's everybody's responsibility to protect and care for them."

Lone Moon's thoughts turned to remorse.

What was I thinking, stampeding horses into the night and putting them in danger? What if the warriors hadn't been able to recover them? What if Crow or Pawnee scouts had been close by and had stolen the horses? By trying to pay the boys back, I frightened every person in camp, waking up elders and babies. I should have thought about what might happen. She fell into a troubled sleep.

The elders reprimanded Fancy Moccasins and Rattling Leaf for not being alert. No one believed their story of ghosts spooking the horse herd. Lone Moon and Early Flower noticed the boys torturously plucking cactus needles out of each other's arms, backs, and legs. Lone Moon shuddered, remembering how much it hurt to have those spines pulled out.

"Maybe our trick was a little too mean," she murmured to Early Flower.

⬗14⬖

WAYS OF WOMEN

IT WAS WINTER, and stars seemed frozen in the sky. Everyone spent most of their time inside, mending worn out moccasins and tools, sharpening arrows, or visiting friends around a sputtering fire. Most of their energy went to keeping warm. When men did go out hunting, they often came back unable to see because vivid winter sun reflecting off dazzling white snow made them temporarily blind.

Lone Moon had savored the first heavy snows that softened and transformed the whole landscape. Large dollops of crystal-white snow clung to drooping pine branches. Clumps of snow-covered sagebrush were pillows, and snowdrifts were fluffy blankets to roll in. Fat snowflakes Lone Moon and Early Flower caught on their tongues tasted like icy magic. But as winter dragged on, Lone Moon found each new snowstorm and ensuing cold difficult to endure. She didn't like constant hazy smoke and wet dog smells choking the dim tipi air. *Will spring ever come? I can't wait to smell fresh green grass again or to ride Cloud through wild flowers and budding trees and to feel the warm sun on my skin.*

A cold wind kept Lone Moon and Early Flower inside one day, learning to bead a pair of moccasins and listening to Yellow Bird's advice.

"Respect, Generosity, Compassion, Bravery, Patience, Humility, and Honesty are important virtues for a Lakota woman to practice," she said. "A woman seeks to be industrious like a spider, wise like a turtle, cheerful like a meadowlark, and generous like the sun that shines on every creature. Our people say, what you give you keep, what you keep you lose."

Grandmothers, respected for their wisdom and knowledge, were expected to counsel their grandchildren, especially their granddaughters. Yellow Bird was taking advantage of this chilly winter day, teaching the girls spiritual values of being good women.

"I'm no good at beading," grumbled Lone Moon, swiping away wisps of hair that always escaped her braids and clouded her vision. "It's hard and monotonous; besides, I can barely see in here." Her fingers felt stiff and clumsy. She glanced over at Early Flower's delicate fingers balancing colorful beads on her bone needle and stringing bead after bead in perfect rows. Early Flower was the image of persistence. Lone Moon screwed her face into an aggravated knot. The beads she managed to pick out of the bowl jammed on her needle, and when she jerked them free, they spilled into the wiry hair of the buffalo robe she had wrapped around her lower body to keep warm.

"I don't have enough patience for beading," Lone Moon groused. She flung her moccasin aside.

Laugh wrinkles crinkled around Yellow Bird's eyes. "Oh, you'll learn to be patient with beading, *takoja*. Someday, you will be asked to make a pair of beaded moccasins for your mother-in-law to honor her and to prove you are a capable wife."

"I've watched you training Magpie," Early Flower added. "You have lots of patience with her and also with practicing to shoot an arrow at a grasshopper."

"And your mother is the leader of our quillwork society. Her beading and porcupine quillwork are brilliant," added Yellow Bird for encouragement. "Only the best sewers are invited into that society."

"I'll never be like my *ina*," Lone Moon protested. "I'd rather be outside riding Cloud, playing with Arrow, or picking berries. Training Magpie and shooting arrows is easy compared to beading, and I can't imagine being somebody's capable wife."

Hot tears pooled in her eyes. She felt ashamed of her childish outburst. Will I ever become a good Lakota woman, *Unci?*" she murmured.

Yellow Bird folded Lone Moon into her arms, buffalo robe and all. "It takes time and practice, but someday you will excel in all womanly virtues," she promised. "You've already demonstrated bravery, when you tried to protect your family during Lt. Grattan's attack. And you show generosity by sharing your treasures with Early Flower and taking time to play with small children.

"Yes," added Early Flower. "You spend hours making whistles and toys for little ones. Their eyes light up when they see you coming."

Lone Moon smiled. She felt warm and cozy. Her *unci* and best friend could always make her feel better.

The next morning, Lone Moon could no longer delay going outside to relieve herself in the trees. An arctic wind sucked the breath out of her mouth, and its icy fingers clawed at her cheeks. She seized a rope tied to the tipi and clutched it tightly, following it to the trees. Frozen rope threads bit into her bare fingers. Snow swirled around her in frosty robes; her nostrils contracted with the bitter cold, making it difficult to take in air. Heavy, drifted snow buried the grass; icicles dangling from the tipi smoke holes resembled glass knives. Lone Moon did her business quickly, never letting go of the anchoring rope, and stumbled back through knee-deep snow. Her toes, nose, and fingers tingled like they were covered with frozen cactus spines. She was glad she wasn't old enough to help women strip bark off ice-covered cottonwood trees in order to feed the horses, who pawed crusty snow only to find the grass underneath flattened and dry.

Families had to ration dried buffalo meat and turnips they had gathered last summer. Frequent blizzards kept hunters from finding fresh meat, and the earth was too frozen to dig any roots. Lone

Moon remembered digging turnips with her mother last summer. It had taken a long time to braid their stems into twines, so they could hang them in the hot sun to dry. These ropes of turnips now dangled from bracing poles in their tipi, making it easy to clip off a few to put into stews. The savory smell of buffalo stew simmering promised Lone Moon a nearly full stomach tonight. Yellow Bird cautioned her to save a little extra food back to share with any families that might not have enough. Being generous was highly stressed in Lakota culture.

Lone Moon missed and worried about her *ina*, who was staying in a special tipi preparing to give birth. *This winter has been so long*, she thought. *What if the harsh cold is too much for a newborn baby?*

━━15━━

WARRIOR TALES

THE LINGERING WINTER did have some fun activities. Random people frequently stopped by in the evenings to tell stories about recent events, times past, or silly animal stories. Lone Moon especially loved humorous stories her *lala* told about Iktomi, a spider, and his rival, Coyote. They both tried to fool other animals with their zany pranks but usually ended up being tricked themselves. One of her favorite stories told how Iktomi tricked some ducks into sitting close to him so he could sing his new songs to them. While the ducks listened, he slipped a sack over their heads then prepared a roasting spit over the fire. A delicious smell of roasting ducks soon filled the air. Unexpectedly, two tall trees close to the fire started making noises. Iktomi, being very curious, spun a high web to discover what was causing the noises, but got tangled in twigs and branches. He looked down and saw Coyote eating his ducks and realized he had been duped. *Coyote, not the trees, must have made the noises,* he fumed.

"Please leave me at least one duck to eat, dear Coyote. You'll be too full if you eat them all," Iktomi wheedled.

"Why sure, I'll leave you one." Coyote generously agreed.

But when spider got untangled and down to the firepit, Coyote was gone, and the duck he left was filled with ashes.

"That crafty Coyote fooled me once again," Iktomi seethed.

Crazy Horse always laughed heartily at these silly tales. Although he would never tell stories about himself, others would relate Crazy Horse's brave deeds and his daring leadership. One evening, Lone Moon listened as Little Hawk, the younger brother of Crazy Horse, talked about a fight they had recently with soldiers.

"You should have seen Crazy Horse," Little Hawk bragged for his brother. "He rode to a peak near the fort. When he was sure soldiers could see him, he got off his horse. He raised its front foot, pretending the horse had hurt its hoof. The soldiers, thinking Crazy Horse was alone, immediately raced out to catch him. But he leaped back on his horse and galloped away to a gully where we were hiding. The soldiers chased him right into our trap. None of the soldiers survived our surprise attack. The plan worked exactly like Crazy Horse said it would, and he managed to dodge all their bullets."

Lone Moon's mind flipped back to a huge victory dance after the skirmish Little Hawk had described.

She recalled how warriors danced inside a circle and boasted about their courage in the fight. Crazy Horse stood to one side, preferring not to be the center of attention. Each time a warrior shared a brave deed, onlookers cheered, and drums beat louder. Lone Moon remembered the celebration lasting until dawn.

Crazy Horse, speaking gravely to adults gathered in the tipi, interrupted Lone Moon's memories. "We have tried several tactics with the white soldiers, but nothing works for long. We don't want war with them, but they have broken many treaties made with our Lakota people. They told us no forts would be built in our hunting grounds. But *wasicu* keep intruding into what the treaty states is Lakota territory. We kept our promise to not bother anyone on their *Holy Trail*. But *Great White Father* did not keep his promise. If we don't fight back and protect the traditional lands of our ancestors, I fear *wasicu* will keep invading our land until there's nothing left for us. If we do fight back, many of our warriors may be killed by their big guns. We need guidance from the *Creator* to help with our dilemma. But before we agree on anything, we will consider how this decision will affect our people seven generations from now. This is Lakota way."

The other men nodded in agreement.

Before Lone Moon drifted off to sleep that night, she thought about the words Crazy Horse had spoken. *I wonder why the wasicu didn't do what they promised. Why would they build forts in the middle of our buffalo hunting grounds? Why were so many of them crossing through Lakota territory? Where were they all going on this Holy Trail?*

Her dreams turned into a disturbing nightmare of many colorful horses gimping down a trail with sore feet and soldiers chasing after them with guns longer than tipi poles.

16

A NEW LIFE

LONE MOON, HALF asleep, shook her head trying to clear spider webs of haunting dreams from her brain. Her *ate* was tickling her face with a feather. A proud grin spread across his face.

"Lone Moon, wake up! You have a baby brother and, at last, I have a son!"

Startled into full awareness, her body tingled with hope and excitement. She whipped around in her buffalo robe blanket to face her father. "What?... The baby is alive?... Is it really true?... I have a brother?"

"Yes, he is a strong boy and can cry like a hungry wolf. He looks like a warrior, already," Sky Eagle boasted.

"Is *Ina* okay?" Lone Moon asked with a worried look.

"Yes," Yellow Bird inserted, "Your mother is weak, but her midwife is taking good care of her. Soon you'll be helping your mother with this little one. He must be a hearty one, born in this frigid weather. As soon as you eat breakfast, we'll go see him. We'll take some of those diapers you helped me make from fawn skin and soft cattail fuzz. Let's also bring the *cekpa* we created."

"Okay, good idea. I remember sewing beads on that buckskin pouch. You told me we were making it to protect our baby. You said special prayers while we worked. But I forgot what goes inside of it."

"We will put in part of the baby's umbilical cord along with eagle down and buffalo hair," replied Yellow Bird. "We will attach it to the cradleboard to show how much this baby is loved."

"But why does it look like a lizard?" Lone Moon asked.

"Because the lizard is respected for its swiftness, endurance, and courage." Smiling, she added, "We also believe if the naval cord is thrown away, the child will grow up irritating people by asking too many questions. So, when you are too nosy your *ina* asks you, "*Cekpa oyale he?* Are you looking for your naval cord?" Yellow Bird chuckled and continued, "Remember when you received the *cekpa* at your ten-winter birthday celebration?"

"Yea, I felt so grown up being trusted with it. I keep it safe in my deer skin treasure bag and fasten it onto my dancing dress whenever there is a ceremony. Can we go see the baby now?" Lone Moon was getting impatient.

Her grandmother gathered diapers, *cepka* and a large piece of velvety buckskin, lined with rabbit fur. Lone Moon scampered alongside Yellow Bird, shuffling through deep snow. After tightly closing the birthing tipi door flap behind them, Lone

Moon blinked back brightness of the snow outside and squinted at her mother lying on a buffalo hide pallet. She was propped up with antelope fur pillows and covered in buffalo robes. She looked tired and pale but gave a radiant smile to Lone Moon. "Meet your baby brother."

A wrinkled, red face peered up at her. Its black chokecherry-like eyes riveted on Lone Moon's face.

"*Aiyee,* he is so cute!"

The baby grasped Lone Moon's finger in his little fist. She gently stroked his soft cheeks and straight black hair. Yellow Bird cooed, beaming down at them.

"But, *Ina,* are you all right?" Lone Moon asked, eyes full of concern.

"Yes, I'm fine. Isn't he precious? You're going to be the best big sister ever." Emotion clogged Morning Star's throat and made her voice squeak like a mouse.

Lone Moon, choked with tenderness, couldn't reply. Thankfulness overflowed in her heart, knowing her mother was okay and the baby was healthy.

She found her voice enough to whisper, "He's adorable, I*na.*"

Morning Star nestled the baby close to her chest, encouraging him to nurse. As Lone Moon watched her mother feed him, her heart felt so happy she feared it would burst wide open like a buffalo bladder too full of water. As long as she could remember, she had wanted a brother or sister.

After the baby's tummy was full, Morning Star gently laid him in her daughter's arms saying, "Take him. Hold your *misunkala,* (little brother)."

Lone Moon gazed lovingly down at his miniature face, considering things to teach him and places to show him. She smiled to herself, thinking he probably wouldn't want the doll they had made. Sky Eagle would make him a little bow with arrows. She knew her parents would probably name him after an ancestor, but Lone Moon decided to call him Nunpa. *It's the perfect name. Nunpa is the Lakota word for two and he is the second child.*

The baby squirmed in Lone Moon's lap and started to cry.

"Put your hand over his mouth and pinch his nostrils," her mother instructed in a calm voice.

Lone Moon gasped, "But he won't be able to breathe."

"Don't worry," Morning Star encouraged. "Do it gently for a bit and sing to him softly so he won't be frightened. It's our way to teach babies not to cry. Imagine how a baby's wail could alert our enemies if they were close by. It would put us all in danger."

Lone Moon understood why it was necessary, but she still didn't like to hold his cute nose shut even for an instant. When Yellow Bird told Lone Moon it was time to go and let her mother and baby rest, Lone Moon could barely tear herself away from her new little brother.

"I promise I'll be back soon, little Nunpa. We can play, and I'll tell you funny stories about Iktomi and Coyote. I may bring Early Flower, and she can be a sister for you, too."

Before going to sleep that night, Lone Moon thanked the spirits for her *misunkala* and *ina's* survival. She knew some mothers died in childbirth.

Bringing a baby into the world is the most special thing a woman can do, Lone Moon decided. *Being a girl is better than being a boy, because girls grow up and birth babies. No boy can do that.*

The next morning, bright sunlight warmed the air and softened the snow. Lone Moon peeked in on her mother and brother. Finding them both asleep, she joined boys and girls, who were playing in the snow.

"I bet we can create a better soldier snowman than you can," Lone Moon challenged Fancy Moccasins and Rattling Leaf.

"Okay, we can beat you at anything," the boys boasted. They were eager to prove their prowess over the girls whatever the competition.

Lone Moon and Early Flower rolled big balls of sticky snow and shaped them into sturdy soldier legs. A fat snow belly came next, topped with a smaller snowball head. They made a hat from old leaves and plopped it on its head, added a pinecone nose and straight sticks for arms.

The boys fashioned similar balls of snow into a soldier's body and searched to find small branches for arms and fingers, black rocks for eyes, a buffalo hoof for a nose, and pine needles for a mustache and beard. Rattling Leaf brought a battered soldier hat that Crazy Horse had given him and plunked it on their soldier's head.

"Come see our soldier," the boys said, standing proudly beside their snowman.

"I have to admit your soldier is better than ours," Lone Moon said in good sportsmanship. Early Flower agreed.

"Now, let's have some fun," Fancy Moccasins said, scooping up some melting snow and forming it into a ball.

He lobbed the ice ball at their soldier and knocked his hat off. The girls giggled, molded more snowballs and joined in, demolishing arms, hats, noses, and eyes. Rattling Leaf formed a huge ice ball and aimed it their soldier's legs. The snow soldier plummeted, disintegrating into a smush of snow. The other snowman soon crashed beside it, prompting everyone to laugh hysterically.

17

HOLY TREE CHOPPERS

SNOW ON THE plains melted like hot fat. Crusted winter snows hugging tall mountains thawed, activating tiny streams below to spiral into boisterous rivers. They bellowed and crashed down steep ravines, overflowing their banks to flood lower meadows. Soft green colors appeared everywhere. Smells of chokecherry and plum blossoms infused soft air. Bouncy robins searched for juicy worms to pluck from the warming earth. Melodious songs of meadowlarks promised peace. Spring had arrived at last. Lone Moon skipped with a joy that rose from deep inside her. Soon it would be time for the SUN DANCE!

Everyone seemed happier as they shook off the throes of winter and prepared for spring and summer activities.

"The council has set a time for the Sun Dance," Crazy Horse told Lone Moon one warm day. "The scouts, Hawk Wing, Wolf Ears, and Little Snake, are taking a message to all Lakota bands to meet at Greasy Grass riverbanks for the ceremony."

Lone Moon didn't wait to hear any more. She raced to Early Flower's tipi. "Have you heard?

There's going to be a Sun Dance, and we're all going!"

"Fantastic!" Early Flower grinned. "Let's help our mothers pack, so we can go right away."

It took Crazy Horse's band five sleeps before they reached the Sun Dance site. After helping set up their family tipis, Lone Moon and Early Flower watched a colorful parade of people pouring into the large camp. Each *tiospaye* consisted of elders, children, mothers, fathers, young braves, warriors, and medicine men along with horses, dogs, and overflowing pony carts. Some men wore vibrant headdresses and carried feather-decorated lances. Women wore fancy dresses adorned with beads that gleamed in the sunlight.

"I'm trying to count all the people, but there are so many I keep losing track," Early Flower said.

"Let's go meet them. There must be girls our age in these crowds." Lone Moon skipped ahead, leading the way.

She and Early Flower wandered among cheerful sounds intermingled with sacred songs and prayers of elders. Lone Moon's eyes darted here and there, trying to take in all the activities surrounding her. She shivered with excitement. Tipis were scattered along the river, so the girls could easily walk around greeting uncles, aunts, cousins, and family friends. Their jaws ached from smiling at all the relatives they hadn't seen for a long time. Lone Moon didn't protest when aunties pinched her cheeks and exclaimed over how tall she had grown.

When the girls went back to their families for supper, Morning Star greeted Lone Moon with a huge smile. "Lone Moon, I have some very exciting news. Elders have selected you to be one of four adolescent girls to symbolically chop the *holy* tree and give tribute to a brave warrior."

"Really! I can't believe it's true. Ever...ever since I was little, I've watched older girls in fancy dresses striking the *holy* tree with special axes and speaking in front of all the people." Words reeled out of Lone Moon's mouth in excited spurts. "I always hoped that one day I would be chosen for this honor. And now...now, I'll be one of those girls." She clasped both hands over her chest and squished the grin on her lips into two deep dimples.

"We're so proud of you," Yellow Bird and Morning Star exclaimed in unison, suffocating her in hugs. "Let's start decorating your ceremonial dress right away."

They sewed bright red porcupine quills onto the soft deerskin dress hem directly above the long, leather fringes. The sleeves and yoke were adorned with tiny black, yellow, red, and white oval beads. They added elk teeth and marble-sized jingle bells down the front and sides. The two women worked late, sewing by firelight until it was finished. Lone Moon fell asleep watching them work.

The first thing Lone Moon saw when she awoke was the most beautiful dress she had ever owned. She tried it on before breakfast and immediately whirled around, producing musical tinkling sounds that became louder and louder as she twirled.

Morning Star had a sewing needle in her hand.

"Quit twirling Lone Moon, and stand still. I need to make sure every stitch is perfect." She and Yellow Bird inspected the dress in morning light and made little tucks and stitches here and there until they were satisfied.

Morning Star fussed over Lone Moon, braiding her hair extra tight and applying bear grease to make it shine. And she cautioned over and over, "Now remember, stand erect and walk slowly with your eyes fixed straight ahead. Don't gawk around to see what others are doing. This ritual is about cutting the tree in a sacred manner, so be sure to follow those specific rules we talked about. Have you decided which of our relatives you are going to praise? It is important to acclaim their heroic deeds. Let's go now, the ceremony is about to begin."

An elder had picked out a large, straight cottonwood tree to be used for the Sun Dance center. Lone Moon and the three other girls followed Badger Eyes, who had been designated to lead the procession and count coup on the tree. He attained this distinction by showing compassion to the elderly parents of a warrior killed in battle. A crowd of spectators walked behind the girls, singing honoring songs for fallen warriors. Lone Moon kept her eyes straight ahead as she walked and tried to look solemn.

Badger Eyes struck the tree with his bare hand

then pointed to Lone Moon. She gripped her beaded, feathered axe, took a deep breath to hide her nervousness, then said with pride, "In the last battle, Crazy Horse rode right into soldiers' gunfire, risking his life to pick up a wounded warrior. He brought this man back safely to his family."

She struck a blow with her ornamented axe. People clapped and cheered. The other girls took turns relating courageous feats of their relatives before whapping the tree with their decorated axes. Several young men stepped forward with sharp axes to fell the cottonwood. Women placed their blankets and shawls underneath, so no branches or leaves would touch the ground when it dropped. Once the big tree was down, Crazy Horse and other warriors trimmed its branches and carried it to the camp center. They placed the tree in a deep hole and tamped moist earth around it. Medicine men smudged the tree, chanted prayers, then declared it holy and ready for the Sun Dance.

~18~

SUN DANCE, WIWANYAG WACIPI

"I'M GOING TO have my ears pierced," Early Flower announced, while walking with Lone Moon. "Then I'll be more like you."

Lone Moon flinched, remembering the stinging pain when her ears had been pierced at a previous Sun Dance.

"That's nice," Lone Moon said, turning her head so Early Flower wouldn't see her grimace. "My *lala* told me kids get their ears pierced to help them become better listeners and more connected to their spirit world."

She decided not to tell Early Flower how much it hurt. *Suffering without complaining is part of the Lakota bravery virtue,* she recalled.

"Do you know how the main dancers pierce their bodies for the Sun Dance?" Early Flower asked.

"Not for sure. Let's ask Crazy Horse," Lone Moon suggested.

They found Crazy Horse sitting by his tipi, rewrapping his bow with wet rawhide strings.

He laid it aside and answered their question

candidly,

"The dancers can choose to participate in the Sun Dance in three different ways. Some choose to have their chest pierced by green, sharpened chokecherry sticks, which are inserted under their skin. Long pieces of rawhide cord are looped under the sticks, then tied to the *holy* tree. The men dance toward and away from the sacred tree several times during the ceremony. Eventually, the dancers tug backwards until the sticks yank free from their skin.

Other dancers choose to be suspended by leather thongs attached to their chests with strong tree sticks. Their body weight causes the chest skin to rip, dropping them to the earth. Still others dance while dragging around buffalo skulls hooked onto their backs until the heavy buffalo heads tear the rigid sticks loose from their flesh.

Early Flower's eyes were big. "Wow, that is some sacrifice. Getting my ears pierced with a bone needle is nothing compared to that. But why do they do it?"

"Some of them want to give thanks because their lives were spared in a battle or because they, or someone in their family, have recovered from an illness or injury. All these young men suffer willingly for the good of everyone. We Lakota consider this our most sacred ceremony."

Early Flower and Lone Moon walked silently back to their tipis, each pondering the graphic images Crazy Horse had painted in her mind. Savory smells of buffalo, elk, deer, rabbit, and antelope roasting in flavorful sauces filled their nostrils. Early Flower went to help her mother and other women, who were preparing a feast that would conclude the Sun Dance.

Lone Moon curled up on her buffalo pallet and watched her *ina* finish making some tiny leather figures that would be used for another Sun Dance ritual. Morning Star had been commissioned to create these little buffalo and human shapes to hang in the *holy tree*. She had spent several suns diligently cutting, sewing, and decorating them. When the small forms were completed, Morning Star summoned Sky Eagle to hang them.

Several young warriors gathered around as Sky Eagle hoisted the figures high into the *holy tree* and looped them over a cross bar. He stepped back and gave a signal to begin. Braves jostled each other to shoot arrows at these dangling effigies. They believed if these miniatures were destroyed, many buffalo would be killed, and no enemies would interfere in the next hunt. Bystanders cheered until all the figures were demolished.

That afternoon, the dancing began. Five main dancers had purified themselves by fasting four days, sitting in a sweat lodge, and praying to spirits for strength. Their bodies were painted in ceremonial patterns and colors special to their families. Each carried an eagle bone whistle, which they blew during their dance to attract the great bird's spirit. Dancers winced in agony when an elder pierced their chest on the left and right side, inserted sticks, strung a cord under them, and affixed it to the *holy tree*. When all were ready, the dancers raised their arms praying toward the sun and began their grueling, slow shuffle to and from the tree, dangling their hands in complete surrender. Many voices blended, singing sacred songs, drums beat cadence in grave thumps, accompanied by trilling eagle bone whistles.

People of all ages danced outside the ceremonial circle, allowing plenty of room for the revered dancers. Everyone gazed intently at the sun as they bounced up and down to music. They averted their eyes every now and then to avoid harming them. It hurt Lone Moon's eyes to look directly at the sun, so she only glanced at it a few times while she danced.

Some women and older men, instead of dancing, made sacrifices by cutting small circles of skin from their arms or legs. Morning Star offered a bit of her forearm skin in gratitude for Nunpa's live birth and good health. Even knowing it was Lakota tradition, Lone Moon still shuddered when she saw the raw sore on her *ina's* arm.

Lone Moon joined onlookers who prayed and sang songs of encouragement for the awe-inspiring dancers. Imagining the dancers' torture, Lone Moon trembled, but her heart surged with pride at their courage. Every time they danced close to where she stood, she pressed a pointed arrowhead tighter into her palm, suffering a little hurt along with the dancers in order to share their pain. This was her way of offering thanks for her parents, Nunpa, Crazy Horse, her grandparents, Early Flower, Cloud, Magpie, Arrow, and all other good people and things in her life.

As the sun lowered, the devout dancers strained against their tethers, leaning back as far as they could. Cheers exploded when the sticks finally ripped free from their chests. The dancers collapsed in exhaustion and anguish. Suffering in silence, these martyrs did not cry out. Medicine men carried the young men to a soft bed of sage in the shade. They served these dancers, who had given so much of themselves, pieces of boiled buffalo heart and chokecherry juice before gently cleaning their wounds and applying time-honored medicines. The Sun Dance ceremony was over. It had brought renewed strength to all. Now it was time to feast and celebrate.

Songs of thanksgiving and revival erupted everywhere. Lone Moon heard many exclamations that warmed her heart:

"The sacrifices of those warriors certainly restored my spirits."

"Do you ever remember dancers being so courageous?"

"I have a good feeling that things will be better now."

"My heart feels stronger. My mind is hopeful."

"Maybe the *wasicu* will go away, and life will be normal again."

Lone Moon turned to Early Flower. "After the bad things that have happened lately, we all needed this holy time."

Early Flower simply smiled. She was still speechless after all she had witnessed.

THE BLACK HILLS, HE SAPA

GRADUALLY, SMALL GROUPS drifted away from the Sun Dance site to establish smaller camps where grass and wildlife were more abundant. Lone Moon was sad to see her relatives depart, but kind of glad to get back to quiet and simple ways of her own *tiospaye*.

Crazy Horse led his band to Powder River country, but it was hot and dry there. Hardly any water flowed in the river. People were restless.

"Why don't we all go to *He Sapa* (Black Hills) for a while," Crazy Horse suggested to the council a few weeks later. "It's cooler there, and hunting is good. *He Sapa* is the heart of all things for our people. It will provide a sacred space to pray, relax, and find food."

Nods and enthusiastic smiles cemented the decision.

That afternoon, Crazy Horse told Lone Moon and Early Flower about going to *He Sapa*.

"That's a wonderful idea!" Lone Moon said, dancing in circles. "I haven't been there for so long. I can't wait to wade in ice cold streams and have fish nibble my toes. Or lay in meadows filled with yellow, red, blue, purple, and orange flowers and watch clouds drift by in dazzling blue skies. And there are so many rocky canyons and hushed forests to explore. It's such a beautiful place, I wouldn't be surprised if the *Creator* himself lives there," Lone Moon exclaimed, clutching her fists to her chest and squeezing her body tight.

Early Flower, who had never seen *He Sapa*, was captivated by Lone Moon's descriptions. "Stop" she laughed, "I won't be able to sleep tonight thinking about those amazing things. When can we leave?"

Lone Moon and Early Flower helped their mothers tear down the tipis, placing poles and buffalo hides onto pony drags. Women packed up cooking utensils, extra clothing, and bedding for cool nights ahead. Men packed weapons for hunting and tools for hewing arrow and spear heads. Older boys gathered horses for women and elders, but the two girls had to catch their own ponies. They took ropes and headed for the horse pen.

Magpie sidled up to Lone Moon who managed a quick touch on the end of her silky muzzle before the filly darted away, kicking her heels high in the air. Magpie, along with other young horses not old enough to ride or pull pony drags, would be driven to the new campsite by some young braves.

Lone Moon chased Cloud back and forth around the pen before she finally cornered him and slipped a rope around his neck. She brushed him clean with sage leaves and threw an elk skin blanket on him. Cherry Blossom approached Early Flower, nosing her for a treat. Lone Moon shook her head at the way Early Flower spoiled her pony. Crazy Horse said horses shouldn't be coddled, but Early Flower was soft with all animals.

"You could charm a skunk," Lone Moon laughed good-naturedly at her friend.

Once everything was ready, the tribe moved along slowly, taking time to accommodate young children and old people. Lone Moon and Early Flower rode their ponies alongside pony drags but frequently galloped ahead to investigate a splashing creek, a rocky crevice, or a clump of yellow-green aspen trees.

Trotting out of a deep valley, they viewed rolling land stretching into the horizon. Early Flower yelled, "What is that? It looks like a giant thumb that froze into a rock!"

"That is really strange," Lone Moon said, doing a double-take. "Let's ask Crazy Horse if he'll take us over there."

The girls raced back to the crooked line of people ambling behind Crazy Horse.

"We saw the weirdest rock. Please, oh please take us to see it up close," they begged.

Crazy Horse, wearied from traveling at a turtle's pace, readily agreed.

"You must be talking about *Mato Tipila* (Devils Tower). Follow me. If you can keep up," he challenged, galloping off at a reckless speed.

The girls sped after him, kicking their ponies into high lopes across the plains. Cloud and Cherry Blossom leapt over cactus plants and clattered over loose rocks.

As they neared the gigantic rock it seemed more massive. It was so tall, clouds made shadows on it as they scooted across its flat top. Riding their ponies to its base, they almost fell off, craning their necks, trying to take it all in. Lone Moon squinted her eyes against sun glinting off the whitish-grey sides, stark against an indigo sky. Shadows, black as crows, highlighted deep vertical crevices.

"I feel so tiny next to it," Lone Moon whispered.

"How did it rise straight out of the ground like that?" Early Flower asked in an awed voice. "I have goosebumps being this close to it. It makes me dizzy looking up so far."

The three explorers walked their horses around the tower's circular base, picking their way around piles of boulders littering their path. They noticed the gaping cracks were similar on all sides.

"It took us longer to walk around this giant rock than it would to put up four tipis," Early Flower commented.

"The view on top must be awesome. I wish I could climb it, but its sides are too slick. And I might get lost in those deep cracks," Lone Moon lamented.

"Can you believe how it looms above everything else? I wonder how long it has been here," Early Flower said pushing her lips out in puzzlement.

The trio slid off their horses to rest under an aspen

tree, whose leaves chattered a friendly welcome. Crazy Horse pulled pieces of *wasna* from his pack for their lunch.

"The Cheyenne tell a legend about *Mato Tipila*, which is older than our oldest ancestors," Crazy Horse said. "It goes like this: seven little girls were playing in the forest. A huge grizzly bear, protecting her cub, chased them. The girls stopped to catch their breath for a moment. Mama bear kept charging after them. They leaped onto a large, flat, round rock. As the bear started to grab them, the rock they were standing on suddenly started rising. Up, up, up, so high they could not be reached. The bear was furious and tore at the towering rock with its enormous claws, straining to capture the girls. She clawed so hard it left the vast scratches you see now. But the girls were safe on top, and eventually the frustrated bear lumbered away, growling her disgust. That night spirits lifted these girls into the night sky and turned them into seven beautiful stars."

"Oh, I love that story," Early Flower smiled.

Lone Moon was a little skeptical about the tale, but it did explain things about this spectacular rock, which was way different than anything in the surrounding landscape.

When their families caught up with them, Lone Moon rushed to greet her parents and grandparents. Words tumbled out like waterfalls, "Can you believe this rock! Isn't it incredible? How did it get here? Crazy Horse told us the Cheyenne legend, but what else do you know about it, *Lala*?"

Swift Bear answered in a reverent tone. "This colossal tower has been here before my grandfathers and before their grandfathers. Our ancestors called this rock the birthplace of wisdom and healing. I have been here many times and have used the special powers of *Mato Tipila* to cure sick people. Mighty spirits dwell here. This is a holy place."

The whole *tiospaye* camped under the tower's shield. A full moon caused supernatural reflections to shiver and quiver around the gigantic rock, making its crevices resemble dark, bloody slashes. Yet, Lone Moon slept well under its burly protection.

21

MORE DISCOVERIES

L ONE MOON GLANCED back as the band
continued their journey. The tower appeared
strong and solid in the morning sun like it would
always be there, guarding Lakota land.   After
traveling all day on horseback, they camped that
night on Spearfish Creek where men used spears
to catch bass in the rushing stream. Lone Moon
and Early Flower clapped every time Crazy Horse
or their *atés* caught a slippery fish. That night, they
stuffed themselves with roasted fish and sweet,
wild raspberries gathered from creek banks.

Crazy Horse led everybody south the next day,
trotting through grassy valleys surrounded by tall
forests. Lone Moon caught a glimpse of Bear Butte
emerging above some trees.

"What is that?" she shouted, urging Cloud to trot
alongside Crazy Horse.

"That is *Mato Paha*, the sacred mountain near
where I was born. See how its shape resembles a
sleeping bear?"

"I think it looks like a big fat tipi with an old dog

sleeping beside it," she giggled.

Crazy Horse shook his head in mock exasperation at her irreverence.

The band traveled two more days before arriving at their destination near French Creek. Lone Moon was glad to slide off Cloud's sweaty back and unwind her stiff legs. Her eyes were drawn to sheer rock cliffs topped by granite boulders balancing precariously above the winding creek. Dense grass and waving wildflowers crammed their camping spot. Fish jumped in the stream. Deer and elk peeked through aspen and oak trees, ready to bound away at the slightest movement. Men readied their hunting weapons and hurried after wild game. Women and girls brushed their tired horses, then hobbled them so they could graze on fresh grass. They set up tipis and sharpened knives, anticipating meat to carve. Lone Moon and Early Flower helped their grandmothers search canyons and gullies for ripe chokecherries and plums. In the next few days, Lone Moon's fingers turned black from picking so many berries, but she didn't mind. The more berries they harvested and dried, the more food they would have come winter.

One hot day, Lone Moon and Early Flower kicked off their moccasins and waded into the icy cold creek. Small stones crunched under their feet, while slimy algae swirled around their bare ankles. Early Flower stomped icy water, spraying Lone Moon's face.

"Hey, quit that, or you'll be sorry."

Early Flower laughed and skittered downstream. Lone Moon collected a handful of tiny, wet rocks, preparing to splash them at Early Flower. But something glittered in her palm. Raking through them with her forefinger, Lone Moon distinguished several shiny pebbles.

"What is it?" Early Flower yelled from a safe distance.

"Some really pretty stones," Lone Moon mused, absorbed with interest. She dug another handful, washed them in clear water, and held them out for her friend to see.

Curious, Early Flower edged closer and scooped up her own handful.

"Oh, they're sparkly! Let's get some more."

They proudly carried several golden pebbles back to show their parents.

"Too soft to make tools or weapons," Sky Eagle muttered, uninterested.

"Too oddly shaped to sew onto a moccasin or a dress," Morning Star added.

Early Flower's parents made similar comments, but the girls still liked the colorful stones and decided to place a few bigger ones in the soft deerskin amulets clasped around their necks. They had no way of knowing how completely their lives would change when General Custer and his soldiers would find similar gold stones in this same creek and start a feverish gold rush to the Black Hills.

Whenever their chores of picking berries, carrying creek water, entertaining Nunpa, and finding firewood were finished for the day, Lone Moon and Early Flower rode Cloud and Cherry Blossom to explore the area around French Creek. One huge granite precipice intrigued Lone Moon; she felt attracted to it somehow. It stood out above other outcroppings and seemed so majestic; it was taller than *Mato Paha.*

Many years later when Lone Moon's son was an old man, a *wasicu,* Korczak Ziolkowski, would begin carving an impressive sculpture of Crazy Horse on that very mountain.

— 21 —

ON THE PEAK

SUN MELTED INTO dusk, but there was still enough light for young people to play whirling bone games in the grass. Lone Moon and Early Flower felt privileged to join in their games and conversations.

"Most of our hunting, berry gathering, arrow chipping, and meat drying are completed. I say we go exploring," Crazy Horse suggested. "Little Hawk and I are planning to climb *He Sapa's* highest peak tomorrow. Does anyone else want to go?"

Lone Moon and Early Flower bobbed their heads at each other, arching their eyebrows in anticipation.

"Can we go, too?" they said in unison.

"If it's okay with your parents, it's fine with me," Crazy Horse replied.

Lone Moon and Early Flower raced to their adjacent tipis to beg permission from their parents.

Lone Moon yelled from her door flap, "My *ina* and *até* said yes!"

"Mine said I could go if your parents let you go!"

Early Flower beamed from her door flap.

Their parents knew the girls would be safe with Crazy Horse, even though the foray would take all day. Their grandmothers packed dried meat, fresh plums, and flasks of water for them to take along.

Crazy Horse and his younger brother, Little Hawk, led several young men, women, and older children uphill on a winding deer trail early the next morning. Arrow tagged along, staying close to Lone Moon, except for the times he bulleted after a jackrabbit that always got away. As they climbed higher, the horses threaded their way over scattered quartz and granite rocks. Sparkling mica gleamed on the sunlit trail. Crazy Horse picked up a piece and demonstrated how to peel it into transparent layers, so thin they could see through them.

"Wow, these are like tiny sheets of ice, only not cold," Lone Moon said, letting a breeze float the delicate mica slices off her open hand as they rode along.

"Look there," Early Flower shouted, pointing north. "Those tall rocks look like bone needles we bead with, only they are giant size!"

Lofty, jagged rocks, jutting into the skyline, did appear to be huge needles complete with crevices for eyes. But steep peaks and large boulders prevented them from riding close to these unusual pillars. Crazy Horse urged them on toward the summit he wanted to explore before dark. He somehow found his way around downed timber, over rugged rocks, through tangled bushes and tall trees.

"Watch for rattlesnakes," one man warned.

When they were almost there, a daunting rock cliff, concealing the mountain's crest, blocked their way. This sheer buttress was impossible to climb on horseback. Crazy Horse dismounted and tied his horse to a tree.

"We'll have to leave our horses here and go the rest of the way on foot," he said. "Follow me."

He walked a few paces then started scaling the vertical rock face.

"Find hand and foot holds in crevices. Always keep at least three holds on the rock," he instructed.

Lone Moon and Early Flower slid off their horses and looked at each other in alarm.

"There's no way," they said at the same time.

"You baby girls stay here, and we men will climb to the top," Fancy Moccasins scoffed, as he easily scaled the rock.

That was all it took to prompt the two girls to begin their ascent. They grabbed for cracks and bumps on the rocks and hoisted themselves little by little until they were so high it made them dizzy to look down. The sun was hot, causing perspiration to trickle down their backs. The rough, craggy surface scraped their knees and elbows, but they wouldn't stop climbing. Lone Moon's arm muscles ached, and her fingers were cut and bleeding. She looked over at Early Flower, whose face was raspberry red with fatigue.

"We can make it. We're almost there," Lone Moon panted.

A strong arm grabbed each of the girls and hauled them over the top ledge. Crazy Horse had rescued them. They collapsed on the jagged surface, too exhausted to move until they heard excited shouts.

"Come look. This view is amazing. I can see *Mato Paha!*"

"*Aiyee!* I've never seen this far before. And rock outcroppings bulge out everywhere."

"Those needle rocks we thought were so tall look miniature from way up here."

"If I squint, the badland plains where the sun rises are barely visible."

Lone Moon and Early Flower scrambled to their feet and gazed, astounded at the expansive land spread beneath them. Lone Moon slowly let out the breath she didn't realize she was holding.

"I bet we can see clear to Powder River!" Lone Moon said taking in the 360-degree view.

"Maybe to Ft. Laramie," Early Flower suggested, shading her eyes as she peered out over the vast area. "Look how hills below us are heaped together like the backs of stampeding buffalo."

Crazy Horse looked pensive as he viewed sprawling tree-covered landscapes and protruding granite rocks below him. He was silent and seemed lost in contemplation. His eyes wavered as they focused on the distant horizon. *Is Crazy Horse having a vision into the future?* Lone Moon questioned in her head, watching his face closely.

Finally, Crazy Horse came back to the present, shaking his head as if to clear his mind. His slumped shoulders and dull downward stare caused everyone to pause and listen intently to his vision.

He spoke with a thick tremor in his voice. "Spirits have shown me what is coming. This place where we are standing will have great spiritual meaning for Lakota people in ages to come. Many visions will be received here, some to my young cousin, Black Elk, who has not yet been born."

"However," Crazy Horse paused for a heavy moment, "*wasicu* will come and take *He Sapa* for themselves." He made a sweeping gesture with his arms to include all the land.

No one spoke. Early Flower's face was ash colored. Lone Moon's stomach felt queasy. *How could this be true? People can't own lands. Mother Earth belongs to everyone.*

"But generations from now," Crazy Horse continued, "our people will often climb this high peak to pray. Today, let us take courage. Notice how the horizon makes a complete circle around us. Our ancestors called this the *sacred hoop*. It is holy, it is *waste* (good). There is no beginning and no end; it goes on forever and includes every person and thing."

22

THE CAVE SCARE

CRAZY HORSE SECURED ropes from atop the rock wall, so the girls easily descended by rappelling down. They asked Crazy Horse if they could spend some extra time collecting sparkling mica to show their parents.

"Okay, but others need help getting down this mountain before sundown. I'll leave Fancy Moccasins and Rattling Leaf as your escorts. You four can easily catch us before we reach the first creek."

Lone Moon wasn't pleased to have the boys stay with them, but she agreed knowing Crazy Horse wouldn't leave Early Flower and her by themselves. Leading their horses, the girls hurried to pick up some of the shiny, unusual rocks. The young braves ambled behind them, scowling with impatience.

"I bet you girls are too scared to go into that cave over there," Fancy Moccasins goaded to relieve his boredom.

"We're not afraid. It's you two who are scared to go in," Lone Moon sneered.

"We went in there this morning on our way up," Fancy Moccasins bragged. "In fact, Rattling Leaf accidently left his hunting arrow at the end of that cave, right Rattling Leaf?"

"What? Um...oh yea. I...I must have dropped it," Rattling Leaf stuttered prompted by Fancy Moccasins' wink. Suspecting the girls were somehow responsible for the ghost-in-the-corral trick, the young braves had been waiting for a chance to get even.

"I'll bet you a braided rope halter you won't go in," Fancy Moccasins dared Lone Moon.

"Oh yea, watch us," Lone Moon responded, thinking how nice a new halter would look on Cloud.

"But you have to prove you went clear to the back. If you bring out the arrow, I'll braid the halter, okay?"

"Agreed," Lone Moon answered, bobbing her head in defiance.

Early Flower's eyebrows shot up, and she stared at Lone Moon in alarm. *Had she lost her mind*?

But Lone Moon had already tied her pony to a tree and was pushing aside bushes obscuring the entrance. Still reluctant, but being a loyal friend, Early Flower tied Cherry Blossom alongside Cloud and followed Lone Moon. Two nervous girls stepped into the cool, dank interior, tripping over each other's feet, neither one wanting to go first. Arrow trailed close by their heels, his ears alert for danger.

"Are you sure we should do this?" Early Flower's voice quavered.

"I'm scared too, but we're not backing down from their challenge," Lone Moon said with a resolute look.

With each tentative step, light from the cave's mouth dwindled dimmer and dimmer, while their fears grew larger and larger. Each footstep echoed in fearsome silence. They cowered at strange shadows that seemed to be expanding and moving with them along the cave walls.

"Did you hear that?" Early Flower simpered, crouching behind Lone Moon. Every sound magnified her fright.

"It was likely a mouse scurrying by. He's probably more scared than we are," Lone Moon replied, trying to make her voice sound brave.

"AAAAH!" Something clipped Lone Moon's ear. She shrieked, jumped into Early Flower, nearly knocking her down. Both girls squealed, flinging their arms over their heads and running backwards. Frantically, they swiped at empty air to ensure the creatures were gone.

"Wh...what...was...that?" Early Flower squeaked.

"It must have been...bats," Lone Moon said swallowing rapidly. I...think...they're gone now."

"Let's leave this scary cave, Lone Moon," Early Flower begged, scraping her palms against her skirt.

"No, we can't quit and let the boys win. Come on, we must be almost at the end. We'll grab the arrow and run back fast as we can." Lone Moon's shaky voice betrayed her fright, but she doggedly stepped forward. Early Flower, jamming her hands into her armpits, obeyed.

It was completely silent again, and so dark they couldn't see their own feet. Clasping each other's arm in a solid grip, the girls crept forward. A drip of icy, cold water from the cave roof stung Early Flower's neck.

"YEOW!" she screamed, careening into Lone Moon.

"Early Flower, settle down," Lone Moon pleaded, biting the inside of her cheek, tasting blood.

They fumbled onward, clenching hands, using their free hands to grope cold, slick sides of the narrow cave. Around a corner, the cave widened into a small room. A wee light filtered through a crack in the high ceiling. Early Flower glimpsed a vague form.

"There's something up there!" she squawked, shaking uncontrollably.

Arrow growled low in his throat then started barking frantically. Springing between the girls, he knocked Early Flower to one side. A terrifying, eerie cat scream flash-flooded the cave when the mountain lion pounced on Lone Moon, ripping open her shoulder muscle with his razor-like claws. Flying backwards from the unexpected impact, her head slammed against the cave floor. The lion's body crushed air from her lungs; its breath reeked of death.

Early Flower screeched, "HELP, HELP. SOMEONE, HELP!"

In an instant, Fancy Moccasins and Rattling Leaf reached them. Arrow was snarling and snapping at the lion, trying to distract him. The lion roared and lashed his deadly claws at the dog, who dived out of his reach. Fancy Moccasins leapt onto the lion, stabbing it over and over with his sharp knife.

"Take that, and that, and that, you beast," he bellowed. Then in a quaking voice he yelled, "Rattling Leaf...Get Crazy Horse...Run...Fast!"

Lone Moon, semi-conscious, attempted to scoot away from the heavy animal, but was pinned beneath its weight.

"Don't try to move! I'll roll him off you," Fancy Moccasins panted. "Rattling Leaf has gone to get Crazy Horse."

Her shoulder screamed in pain. Blood spurted into a pool of sticky, warm goo beside her. A dreamlike stillness enveloped her mind before she lost consciousness. Lone Moon's last thought was she'd never see little Nunpa or her mother again.

Crazy Horse hurtled to Lone Moon's side. He held his fingers against her throat, making sure she had a heartbeat then examined the gaping slashes on her shoulder.

"Fancy Moccasins, ...Go...Grab...aspen leaves. Bring them immediately... Hurry!" Crazy Horse's voice rasped with anguish. He cradled Lone Moon's pallid face in his hands.

Arrow whimpered and licked Lone Moon's face.

Early Flower sagged against the wall, crumpling in sobs.

Moments later, Fancy Moccasins returned, both hands clutching leaves. He thrust them at Crazy Horse.

"Is she still alive? Is...is she going to make it?" he stammered.

Crazy Horse soaked the leaves in lion's blood and plastered them onto Lone Moon's yawning gashes. The stupor in her eyes was a mud puddle of agony melting into nothingness.

Lone Moon woke long enough to realize Crazy Horse was carrying her into the family tipi. Her mother and grandmother hovered over her, crying. A medicine man applied herbs and poultices to her wounds. He insisted Lone Moon swallow a ladleful of bitter herbal tea. She gagged it down and almost immediately fell into a deep sleep.

Thanks to her *ina* tenderly changing the dressings on her ragged cuts day after day, Lone Moon slowly recovered.

Basking in the sun one warm day, Lone Moon sat by her tipi. Arrow lay protectively beside her. Her right arm and shoulder were wrapped tightly to her side, but she was able to wiggle two fingers a little, even though needles of pain shot up her arm. Early Flower perched near Lone Moon, beading. She waited on Lone Moon like a robin caring for its young. Six times a day, Early Flower lugged a bladder bag of ice-cold water from the creek, so Lone Moon would have fresh, cool water at all times. She kept a wooden bowl overflowing with hand-picked berries and bits of dried buffalo liver. The medicine man said these foods were important for healing. Lone Moon appreciated Early Flower's constant chatter. It took her mind off the pain and made dreary hours of sitting more bearable. Lone Moon couldn't wait to get on Cloud again and gallop freely over the prairies.

Her grandmother had scraped and tanned the lion's hide until it was as soft as a snake's belly. The pelt was transformed into a light-brown piece of leather. Yellow Bird proudly presented it to Lone Moon.

"Oh, *Unci*," Lone Moon said, her voice going soft and gentle. "It's beautiful, and I know how hard you worked to make it for me, but do you mind if I give it to Fancy Moccasins? He deserves it for saving my life. All I want is this halter for Cloud." Lone Moon patted the splendid, hand-braided halter Fancy Moccasins had made for her.

"Of course, you can give it to him. I see you are learning the virtue of generosity, putting others before yourself."

Fancy Moccasins visited her every day, bringing little gifts he had made. He apologized over and over for daring her to enter the cave. During one visit, Fancy Moccasins took a deep breath and confessed, "Uh, I hope you won't hate me forever, Lone Moon, but I need to tell you something." He paused, took another notched breath and continued, "um, Rattling Leaf and I had never been in that cave before you and Early Flower went inside. We made up the story about leaving the arrow to trick you girls. We tracked close behind you and made scary noises and threw little rocks by your feet. But when I heard the screams, I ran faster than I ever have and got there immediately after that rotten lion knocked you down. I unsheathed my knife lightening quick and must have stabbed him forty times. I was so scared and angry at myself for urging you to go in there. Please forgive me, Lone Moon. I'd rather die a hundred times than see you get killed. I was so relieved when you opened your eyes."

Fancy Moccasins' face rumpled with sorrow, and his eyes implored her. Seeing this different side of him, Lone Moon couldn't help but forgive him. She knew he hadn't meant anything harmful to happen.

Her face softened. "I never have thanked you for saving my life. If you hadn't acted so swiftly, I wouldn't be here right now talking to you. I forgive you, and I also forgive the mountain lion, who was, after all, only protecting his home. We should not have intruded into his cave."

23

CAVE SCARE TWO

A LIGHT MIST WAS falling, not really rain, but causing enough moisture so Lone Moon couldn't take Nunpa outside to play. The weather had turned cooler, sometimes decorating grass with frost on early mornings. Lone Moon was restless in the stuffy, cramped tipi. Nunpa was fussy. Early Flower was sick with a cold.

"Lone Moon, I need you to watch the baby while I go to my women's quilling and beading society," Morning Star said. "Your *até* and *lala* are hunting with Crazy Horse, and your *unci* is visiting relatives. Please don't let him out of your sight even for the swish of a horse's tail. You know how fast he crawls and could easily get into the fire pit. And be sure to keep him warm and dry. I won't be gone too long."

"Okay. Have fun." Lone Moon grabbed Nunpa's chubby hand. "Wave bye-bye to *Ina*."

Lone Moon rummaged around the tipi looking for something to occupy her and the baby. *There's nothing to do in here.*

An idea popped into her head. Turning to her

misunkala, she said, "I'll bundle you into the cradleboard, cover you with a warm deerskin blanket, and carry you to my secret hiding place. It will be dry in there, so you can crawl to your heart's content while I work on fixing up my new hideaway. We'll both be happy."

Nunpa gave her a toothless grin. Lone Moon gathered toys, food, and extra blankets. She tried lifting them plus the baby, snuggled in his cradleboard. "Ouch!" she cried. Darts of pain shot through her still tender shoulder wounds from the mountain lion attack. She dropped to one knee setting the heavy load down. "You are getting too big, Nunpa."

Now what?... I know, I'll take Nunpa first and quickly come back for the other stuff.

She hoisted baby and cradleboard, holding them tightly against her left shoulder. Lone Moon splashed through the icy creek, clambered up the limestone cliff, and pushed aside cedar branches that hid the cave opening. She placed Nunpa inside, facing backwards so no rain would splash his face.

"There, it is nice and dry here, and you are safely tucked into your cradleboard. Don't move. I'll run fast and grab our stuff, okay? I'll be back before you know I've left."

She raced to the tipi, grabbed their things, and charged back up the cliff, strewing rocks in her wake. She crawled into the cave opening, gulping breaths of air. "See, I told you I'd be right ba..."

Her stomach lurched. She stifled a scream. The

hair on her arms stood straight up.

A RATTLESNAKE! NEXT TO NUNPA.

The snake slithered a little closer to Nunpa's toes, sliding a forked tongue in and out of its slimy mouth. Frantic, Lone Moon abandoned all reason. The only viable weapon nearby was the baby's buffalo hoof toy. She grabbed it with her left hand and hurled with all her might...She missed. The rattlesnake, rattled its long tail, coiled, and struck the toy that rolled alongside it.

Nunpa smiled and babbled, oblivious to any danger. Lone Moon's mouth was dry as old leather, and her legs shook. Sticky sweat ran down both sides of her face.

Don't panic... Save Nunpa. Horrifying thoughts raided her brain. *What if there's a den of rattlesnakes, hundreds of them in this cave?* Lone Moon pictured tangled masses of snakes crawling all over her and the baby, mouths open, poison dripping from their fangs, their forked tongues touching her face and infesting her hair. She forced these loathsome visions from her mind. *I...must... stay... calm.*

Keeping her eyes trained on the snake, Lone Moon felt behind herself, careful not to make any sudden moves that would startle it. Her hand identified cedar branches piled near the cave's mouth. She eased one branch free. Creeping to the cradleboard, she got close to the snake's head. She wiggled the branch, attempting to divert its attention away from Nunpa.

The rattlesnake whipped its head around lightning quick and struck the branch, barely missing Lone Moon's fingers. Her heart lurched. Energy drained from her body, buckling both knees. She swallowed hard, took a raggedy breath, but kept backing and jiggling the branch. The serpent slithered after her, hissing and striking. She continued shaking the branch, slinking further into the narrowing cave. The cave walls started closing in on her, but her plan was working!

Until... CLUNK! Lone Moon's back smacked into the rear wall.

Trapped!... Snake still coming!... No escape!

In desperation, she hurled the cedar branch at its face. The snake coiled, striking it twice. Lone Moon tried leaping over the vile creature but tripped on a pointed rock and fell flat on her side. Terror clogged her lungs. She lay still on cold earth, frozen with dread. She was eye to eye with the rattlesnake. One of her long braids splayed dangerously close to its mouth. Her left eyelash brushed the rocky floor. *I don't dare move.*

She couldn't wrench her eyes away from the snake. Its tongue flicked at her. *It's over... The snake is going to strike me... I'm going to die! Is this what I get for disobeying ina and putting the baby in danger? What will happen to Nunpa if I die in this cave? No one will know where to find him.*

She scrunched her eyes shut, gritted her teeth, and prayed to the spirits.

Time passed. It was spookily quiet.

Nothing's happening. The snake hasn't bit me.

Lone Moon squinted through her right eye and saw the snake sidling away from her. She watched in amazement until its rattles disappeared into a vertical crevice.

She shook her head to clear it. *What??? Did...did I see what I thought I saw? Did that snake really crawl away? Am I okay?*

Lone Moon's next thought was of Nunpa. She jumped to her feet, scrambled over loose rocks, fell, scattering dirt and skinning her knees, but kept clawing her way to the front. When she reached the baby, she couldn't believe her eyes. He was sound asleep. Lone Moon squashed him into her arms, cradleboard and all. She rocked back and forth, laughing, blubbering, and thanking the spirits over and over for protecting them from tragedy.

Nunpa woke up, but all he said was, "goo, goo, ga, ga."

Lone Moon laughed, threw the blanket over his head, and lugged him and all their things back in one trip, caring not one bit that her shoulder throbbed with the effort. She was not going to abandon Nunpa again. She undid the cradleboard fastenings, laid her *misunkala* on a blanket, and collapsed beside him, exhausted.

"I'm not telling *ina* or *até* about this incident," Lone Moon said to her baby brother. "I don't ever want to think about it again. I'm not even going to tell Early Flower. I'm so, so glad you can't talk yet,

Nunpa."

She recalled the counsel Uncle Bear Claw had given her after the mountain lion attack. *"Spirits saved you once again. Be grateful always for good in your life. Your duty now is to be levelheaded and wise, as an example to others."*

"So much for listening to my uncle," she said, biting her lower lip and rolling her eyes.

— 24 —

POOF, THEY WERE GONE

WINTER PASSED WITH unusual mildness. But an early spring storm dumped wet, heavy snow that reached clear to horses' bellies. Lone Moon was stranded in the tipi watching Nunpa while he napped. She started reliving her past misadventures. *I should have known how dangerous it was for me and Cloud to charge off helter-skelter and count coup on a buffalo. And I could have gotten us all killed when I opened the tipi door flap and tried to shoot a soldier. I thought pulling the ghost trick on the boys would be funny, but they could have gotten seriously hurt, and everybody would have suffered if the horses had been stolen. It was dumb of me to fall for Fancy Moccasins' dare to go into that mountain lion cave. I should have known it was a trick, besides I put my best friend in danger. But the worst thing I did was to take my sweet misunkala into that rattlesnake cave just because I was bored.* She shook her head recalling all the narrow escapes she had survived. *I must start thinking before acting, like my elders have told me. That's what Crazy Horse always does.*

Morning Star and Yellow Bird interrupted her thoughts, stumbling into the tipi with armloads of wood, laughing as they shook soggy snow from their buffalo robes.

"Brrr, it's freezing cold out there, but I have to go out again to cut some meat off the deer your *até* shot this morning," Morning Star said.

"I'll stir the fire and sharpen knives to slice the meat into strips for frying," Yellow Bird replied. "Oh, and if it's not too much trouble, would you mind bringing in the deer hide before it gets too frozen? I'd like to start processing it to make new moccasins for everyone."

Lone Moon got up to help her grandmother. "I'm lucky to be in this family. You and *ina* work so hard making sure we keep warm and have enough to eat and plenty of clothes to wear. And *até* and *lala* hunt for meat and always protect us. And, somehow you make working fun."

"It's all part of being a good Lakota person. We take care of each other. Look at you, jumping up to help me. You are learning our ways of life," said Yellow Bird with a tender smile.

Lone Moon felt a rush of happiness in her heart. *Maybe I am starting to grow up and be more responsible.*

Almost overnight the weather changed, and spring arrived. Grasses greened and purple crocuses poked their lavender noses through dry pine needles. Lone Moon loved this magical time of year when daylight lasted longer, birds returned from wherever they had gone, and baby animals appeared everywhere.

Lone Moon was carrying cumbersome water bags when she spotted a person riding toward camp. She instantly knew it was Crazy Horse. As he got closer, she noticed a smile wider than the Powder River replacing his usual solemn expression.

He vaulted off his horse and stuck his lance in the ground, a signal for all to gather and listen. An immediate crowd assembled around him. "The soldiers have moved out of their fort!" He grinned, pumping his fists in the air. "Scouts told me the troops loaded all their belongings in wagons and disappeared over the big plateaus where the sun rises."

Hoots, yells, and laughter exploded. People bumped shoulders and hugged each other. Lone Moon and Early Flower danced in circles arm-in-arm.

Three scouts came into camp later that afternoon and told more details about the soldiers' departure.

Little Snake's eyes glowed as he spoke, "We watched the soldiers for a long time to be sure they were leaving for good, then we rode to the fort. We picked up some things they left behind, thinking they might be useful." He unrolled his blanket and dumped some dented tin cups and plates, pieces of rope, an iron kettle, a rusty pair of spurs, a few battered leather hats, bent stirring spoons, and boots with holes worn through the soles.

Wolf Ears continued, "Hawk Wing lit some sagebrush torches. We held them against bottom poles supporting the fort. The dry wood burned slowly at first, but soon it burst into flames. It wasn't long until the whole fort was blazing. It's a long way off, but you might still be able to see the smoke."

"The best part," Hawk Wing interrupted, "we met four Cheyenne scouts who said forts in their area were also abandoned. They claim there is a great war going on among *wasicu*. They are fighting their own brothers. That's probably why the soldiers have left. Who knows how long the *wasicu* war will last, but soldiers won't have any forts if they do return."

The people were puzzled about why *wasicu* would fight each other, but glad soldiers were occupied with something other than interfering in their lives.

Lone Moon and Early Flower rode onto the prairie looking for signs of a fort burning. Far off, black feather-like smoke darkened the evening sky and billowed over the plains. The girls watched until the wind snatched it all away.

"A long time ago," Lone Moon reminisced, "when Crazy Horse and I were at a pond, I noticed a cloud that looked like an eagle feather. I wondered if it meant good fortune. Maybe it did."

"Good riddance!" Early Flower said, making a mock soldier salute. "I hope we never see another *wasicu.*"

"Yea," Lone Moon said. "Hopefully, it will be peaceful and fun like it was before the soldiers came. Maybe Crazy Horse will have more time to spend with us."

But her next breath hiccupped a wisp of doubt.

TOUGH QUESTION

L ONE MOON HADN'T seen any signs of white soldiers for many moons. People seemed at ease. They joked, played pranks on one another, and talked about going back to the old ways.

One evening, Lone Moon and Crazy Horse walked up a knoll to watch the sunset. Tall prairie grasses glinted in golden waves as far as they could see. The last sun rays lit bare hilltops behind them, accentuating every rock and yucca plant. Three deer in the meadow, with grass trailing from their mouths, cocked their heads and studied Lone Moon and Crazy Horse. One of them, deciding it was safe, drank from the creek. The western horizon ripened from mellow orange to rich gold tinged with red and streaked with knife-like, purple slashes. Soft clouds in the east turned rosy pink as if jealous of the colorful sunset. Lone Moon and Crazy Horse watched until the scene wilted into a bluish hue. A bald eagle circled low, hunting for rodents. The first star peeped out like a shy fawn peering between its mother's legs.

Lone Moon loved this part of the day. Standing tall and straight with a slight breeze blowing her long, silky braids away from her face, she felt contented and free. Yet, something nagged at her heart. The sunset reflected honesty into her spirit, urging truth to come forth. The rattlesnake incident jangled stubbornly in her mind like an unfinished story. She had never told anyone about it. She decided to tell Crazy Horse.

He listened without interrupting while she nervously told him all the details.

"I am glad you recognize it was a heedless decision to take Nunpa into the cave. You acted wisely to lure the snake away from him without considering the danger to yourself. You show maturity by being able to admit your mistakes. That means you are gaining wisdom. Spirits have come to your aid many times. What have you learned from them?"

"I have been thinking about that. I believe I'm learning how important it is to stop and think before doing something, especially if it may be dangerous. But changing the way I normally do things is hard," Lone Moon said with a sigh.

"I agree. It is difficult to alter our human natures. But change will always be a part of life. The wise ones keep what is good about themselves, but are willing to try new ways. We don't allow others to transform who we are, but we accept changes that may make our lives easier, safer, and better for those around us."

Lone Moon exhaled a long breath. It felt good to

loosen the guilt she had been carrying and to hear practical comments from Crazy Horse. What he said made sense to her.

Chirping crickets greeted the dusk, and a spicy fragrance rose from the meadow. An innate awareness that she was one with everything engulfed her spirit. Crazy Horse smiled at her, and she guessed he was feeling the same way. As darkness settled over the plains, a troublesome fear haunted her.

"Do you think the soldiers will come back?" Lone Moon asked, goosebumps rising on her arms.

Crazy Horse shrugged his shoulders and sighed. "Some questions have answers as tangled as tumbleweeds."

She shivered, but not from cold. *Was that a soldier's bugle echoing on the wind?*

AFTERWORD

In following years, the *wasicu* did return in wagon trains that stretched as far as Lone Moon's eyes could see. Men, women, and children flooded the area bringing all their possessions with them, including many livestock. Some settled on land that treaties had allotted to the Lakota, and some went further west. Lone Moon's life changed forever in ways she never imagined. Even Crazy Horse could not save the Lakota people's way of life.

AUTHOR'S NOTE

People may ask, what qualifies me, a white woman, mother, teacher, and school principal, to write about Crazy Horse. This my response:

My inner being feels connected with Lakota people. The first seven years of my life were spent in Wyoming, running free and riding my pony among sagebrush and prickly pear cactus in rough Powder River country. My great aunt showed me how to rub sage leaves between my palms and breathe in its calming blessing. When we moved to a small town in South Dakota edging the Black Hills, I played and dreamed under the cottonwood trees that surrounded our home and the nearby Cheyenne River. Our family frequently picnicked in the mountains, affording me a chance to catch glimmers of ethereal native voices whispering in the tops of tall ponderosa pine trees. A spiritual spark of kinship inflames my soul whenever I drive or hike through this western land that Crazy Horse and the Lakota people loved so deeply.

Being familiar with South Dakota Social Studies curriculum, I noticed a lack of native narrative in our history books. My intent is that this book will be used as a supplement for middle grade studies of American history, so that children of all ethnicities may understand and empathize with the struggles, joys, and beauty of Lakota culture.

While visiting Crazy Horse Memorial Museum a few years ago, I had a sense that Crazy Horse spoke to my heart. It seemed like he was encouraging me to write a children's book about him and his way of life. Because there is limited written history about Crazy Horse, I read whatever I could find, trying to bring an authentic yet entertaining story to my audience. I hope this book will capture the truth about sacred Lakota life in the mid nineteenth century. These people were the original Americans. They only took from Mother Earth what was needed to survive and continuously gave back to nature. The following endeavor is my small way of promoting justice and apologizing for the atrocities committed against Lakota people.

It was necessary to exercise literary license to make Lone Moon's fictitious existence come to life, but this story is as historically accurate as my research from native and non-native resources afforded. The book may not always be chronologically correct, and I had to simplify events due to the age and innocence of the intended reader. Crazy Horse lived in a chaotic era. There are myriad written and oral perspectives of the actual history that took place. In order to form your own opinion of these turbulent times, I recommend reading the resources listed in my bibliography.

GLOSSARY OF
LAKOTA WORDS USED IN STORY

Aiyee - Expression of surprise or joy

Akicita - Men in charge of policing the camp

Até (ah-Day) - Father

Cepka(chay-k'pah) - Buckskin pouch shaped like a lizard

Cepka oyale he - Are you looking for your naval cord?

Creator – God, source of all things

Great White Father - President of the United States

Hanble(hahn-blay) - Vision

Hanbleceya (hahn-blay-chay) - Vision Quest

He Sapa (ghay-sah-pah) - Black Hills

Holy Tree - Cottonwood tree, center of Sun Dance ceremony

Ieska - A translator of Lakota language

Ina (ee-nah) - Mother

Lala (lah lah) - Grandfather

Mas'ke - Hello

Mato Paha - Bear Butte

Mato Tipila - Devils Tower

Misunkala - Little brother

Nunpa (nuem-pah) - The number two, name of Lone Moon's brother

Pilamiyaye (pee-lah-mah-yah-yea) - Thank you

Takoja(dah-koh-zjah) - Grandchild

TaSunke Witko - Crazy Horse

Tatanka (dah-dahn-kah) - Bison or buffalo

Tiospaye - Family unit

Unci (uhn-chee) - Grandmother

Wasicu (wah-shee-chue) - White person

Wasna (wah-snah) - Pemmican, chokecherries and buffalo meat

Wasté(wah-shday) - Good

Wiwanyag Wacipi - Sun Dance

BIBLIOGRAPHY

Ambrose, Stephen E. *Crazy Horse and Custer.* Anchor Books. New York. 1996.

Bauer, Marion Dane. *Land of Buffalo Bones. The Diary of Mary Ann Elizabeth Rodgers, an English Girl in Minnesota.* Scholastic Inc. New York. 2003.

Bray, Kingsley M. *Crazy Horse, A Lakota Life.* University of Oklahoma Press: Norman. 2006.

Brown, Vinson. *Great Upon the Mountain, story of Crazy Horse, legendary mystic and warrior.* Macmillan Publishing Co., Inc. New York. 1971.

Decory, Jace. *CEPKA.* Handout for Black Hills University class. 2007.

Denig, Edwin Thompson. *Five Indian Tribes of the Upper Missouri.* University of Oklahoma Press. 1961.

Eubank, Nancy. *Roots. The Dakota.* Minnesota Historical Society. St. Paul, MN. Vol. 12. No. 2/ Winter 1984.

Gregory, Kristiana. *Jenny of the Tetons.* Harcourt Brace Jovanovich. New York City, NY. 1989.

Guttmacher, Peter. *Crazy Horse Sioux War Chief.* Chelsea House Publishers. Philadelphia, PA. 1994.

Hardorff, Richard G. *The Death of Crazy Horse.* University of Nebraska Press. Lincoln, NE. 1998.

Marshall, Joseph M. *The Journey of Crazy Horse.* Penguin Books. 2004.

Marshall III, Joseph M. *The Day the World Ended at Little Bighorn.* Viking Penguin. 2006.

Matson, William B., and The Edward Clown Family. *Crazy Horse the Lakota Warrior's Life and Legacy.* Gibbs Smith. Layton Utah. 2016.

McGaa, Ed, J.D. Eagle Man, *Crazy Horse and Chief Red Cloud.* Four Directions, Publishing. 2005.

Milton, John R. *Crazy Horse.* Dillon Press, Inc. Minneapolis, Minnesota. 1974.

Neihardt, John G., *When the Tree Flowered.* Macmillan. 1951.

Neihardt, John G., *Black Elk Speaks.* University of Nebraska Press. 1979.

O'Brien, Dan. *The Contract Surgeon*. Houghton Mifflin Company. Boston & New York. 1999.

Powers, Marla N. *Oglala Women*. University of Chicago Press. Chicago & London. 1986.

Robbins, Ken. Thunder on the Plains. Anteneum Books for Young Readers. 2001.
Sajna, Mike. Crazy Horse: The Life Behind the Legend. Castle Books. Edison, NJ. 2000.

Sneve, Virginia Driving Hawk. Lana's Lakota Moon. University of Nebraska Press. Lincoln, NE. 2007.

Terry, Michael Bad Hand. Daily Life in a Plains Indian Village 1868. Clarion Books. New York, New York. 1999.

White Hat, Albert. Life's Journey ZUYA: Oral teachings from Rosebud. The University of Utah Press. Salt Lake City, UT. 2012.

www.warpaths2peacepipes.com/native-american-life/counting-coup.htm

www.aktalakota.stjo.org. Akta Lakota Museum and Cultural Center, St. Joseph's Indian School. Chamberlain, SD.

Made in the USA
Columbia, SC
18 January 2022

54049635R00088